COMA TALK

COMA TALK

by
Dana Pride

Everlasting Publishing
Yakima, Washington
USA

Coma Talk

by
Dana Pride

Cover Art by Jahla Brown

This book is a work of fiction.
The persons in this book are fictional
characters, although the dreams are real.

ISBN-13: 978-0-9983858-4-6

First Edition
Everlasting Publishing
P.O. Box 1061
Yakima, WA 98907

I would like to dedicate this book to my family, always supportive of everything I do, and to the people who have unknowingly inspired characters in this story. Thank you so much.

I would also like to thank God for making all things possible.

What happens when a life is changed completely by seemingly random circumstances? Some people think nothing is random and everything happens for a reason, or is part of God's plan.

When things begin to go the way you think they should go, how far will you go to be sure they go your way? What are you willing to do?

COMA TALK

MANDY

"It was a beautiful service," I say to my husband as he starts the car. We are all jazzed up. We just came out of a revival service. I look behind me to be sure the boys have their seat belts fastened as we begin our drive home, nearly two hundred miles. My husband skillfully maneuvers through the thick Seattle traffic.

"Dad, you did good tonight," Caleb, one of our 10-year-old twins says.

"Why, thank you, Son," my husband says graciously. I look at his profile, still amazed after our 17 years together that he chose me to be his wife. I hadn't completely given up on men when we met, but since I was in my 30s at that time, with no real prospects – ever – I was beginning to doubt that God really had a man reserved for me. The fact that I was attracted to him and he to me had been the first sign that maybe he was the one. As I got to know him and saw the amiable way he treated people and the way he loved people, I knew he was my type: loving, kind and friendly. He was the kind of man I didn't know existed outside of romance novels and chick flicks. The way he pursued me, making an effort to make me his own, without me having to call him or chase him or try to show up where he might be, let me know he really wanted to be with me, that our attraction was mutual.

The fact that many other women also wanted him, but he chose me, without any interest in them, was the clincher. He loved me first, and I love him best.

As we are coming to a stop on a one-way street, a fast-moving, gigantic pickup truck makes a right turn into our lane. I instinctively close my eyes, to avoid seeing the inevitable crash.

"Lord Jesus!" my husband cries, as a loud screeching sound drowns out his voice.

I am braced for the impact, which, thankfully and surprisingly, does not come. I open my eyes and see that the truck has skidded to a stop, just inches in front of our car. The driver shakes his fist at us, as if it were somehow our fault he turned the wrong way onto a one-way street. He peels out as he backs up his truck, narrowly missing another car, and continues on his way.

"Are you okay?" I ask the boys, turning around in my seat to see their faces.

They both nod their heads, seemingly oblivious to our near-accident.

"Thank God," my husband says passionately. He is so cool, so relaxed, while my heart is beating wildly. He is an excellent driver, but we both know that only God could have prevented that collision. I am truly thankful. We go a few more blocks before we get on the freeway. Traffic is moving smoothly and after scanning the landscape for any other crazy drivers and seeing none, I begin to relax.

"I'm hungry," Joshua, our other twin says. "Can we stop and get something to eat?"

"You are always hungry," his dad teases.

"We just ate after the service," I remind him, "not even half an hour ago. Didn't you have some chicken and potatoes and gravy and two rolls and green beans and corn and a piece of cake?"

"Yeah, but I didn't get enough," Joshua says. "That mean lady wouldn't let me have seconds."

"You have to wait until everyone has firsts before you can have seconds," Caleb tells him, imitating my voice and repeating a phrase I have often used at church functions where food has been served. I smile with a warmth inside of me, knowing that our sons are learning from us as they grow; and growing fast they are.

"We'll stop and get something to eat when we get down the road a ways," my husband promises.

"The message you preached was really effective," I say, in an attempt to turn the conversation away from food. "I could see that a lot of people in the congregation were touched."

"It was the Spirit of the Lord going forth," he says. "I didn't mean to go in that direction. I had a completely different message ready that I was working on all week, but the Holy Spirit directed me to go another way. We always need to follow the leading of the Holy Spirit, even if we have our own plan in mind."

"Amen!" Caleb and Joshua say together. I hear them slap each other's hands, giving each other a high-five.

"Aaaaaa-men!" my husband repeats, stretching it out for emphasis.

I am so glad he is driving, since darkness is falling, and I am getting sleepy. My eyes are so heavy. I know he must be tired, too. He was up an hour before I was this morning, he had driven all the way to Seattle, we were in service most of the day, he preached the final message of the revival, and now he is driving us home. However, I know his adrenaline is pumping, one of the after-effects of preaching a good sermon to a responsive congregation.

"I'm just going to close my eyes for a few minutes," I tell him. "If you get sleepy, I can drive."

"Just go ahead, my Dear," he says. The hum of the car engine is rhythmic and the motion of the car is soothing, as I let myself go to that other place. I know I am safe, in good hands.

NICHOLAS
Now

Nicholas Robbins's heart was pounding as he parked his car in the hospital parking garage. Everything was finally working out the right way for him, after all his hard work and the things he had endured. The course of his life had clearly led him here, through many detours, but finally right here, to the woman he had loved since they were together in grade school.

He flew up the garage stairs, not bothering to wait for the elevator. As a doctor who had, until recently, worked in this hospital, he knew his way around, and the quickest shortcut to any given area. He took a back stairway inside the hospital so he could sprint up to the intensive care unit, briefly reflecting on the events that brought him here tonight: the fatal car accident, his chance phone call to a colleague, a quick conversation about a patient who was the only survivor of the accident, and the incidental mention of her name: the name of the woman he still loved.

He passed the family waiting area where a couple who were huddled together looked up at him, presumably to discover if he had any news for them, and quickly averted his eyes. He had no news for them. He was here to get his own news.

He approached the intensive care unit and entered boldly. A nurse glanced at him, smiling with recognition, but he dismissed her look as he made his way to his destination. He had permission, he had authority: he was meant to be in this specific place at this particular time.

NICHOLAS
Then

Nick stared at the cutest girl in school, Mandy Foster, as their teacher, Mrs. Graves, told the class to take their reading books from their desks. Nick had been staring at Mandy since second grade started in September when they had been put in the same class. She wasn't like the other noisy girls. She was quiet. She was cute with her short, curly hair, and she was smart. When the teacher called on her to answer a question, she seemed to be as shy as Nick himself was, but she always gave the correct answer.

He looked hard at her, willing her to look in his direction – and she finally did! She was startled to see him staring right at her. She looked away from him quickly and up at the teacher, but he saw the dimples form when she smiled. He saw her cheeks flush, feeling her embarrassment; for this was how he felt every time he saw her, his face hot, his heart warmed and tingly.

Nick's grandparents had met when they were both seven years old, and his grandfather had told him the story about how he had taken one look at his grandmother the first time she had come with her family to his church, and he knew at that very moment that she was the girl for him. It had taken him eight years to convince her, but they got married when they were fifteen years old. They recently celebrated their 40th wedding anniversary.

Nick knew already he wanted to marry Mandy when they grew up, even if it would take eight years – or more – to convince her.

MANDY

I am young, but I am old. I look in the mirror and I see a teenager; yet I know I have grown up and gotten married. My husband is so loving to me, so caring. He is always so calm and patient – I have a lot to learn from him. Is that why God chose him to be in the ministry? Or did he become patient after he answered his call to the ministry? I need to keep my mind on Jesus, to let Him control me, and to be kind and patient to everyone, like my husband is; like Jesus is.

Voices are speaking around me as I am walking down a long hallway. I am directly in the center of the hall, following a straight line painted on the floor below me, and a straight line of fluorescent lights on the ceiling above me. I want to know what the people are saying, but I am compelled to keep moving forward. The hallway must have an end, way down there. I can't see the end. My legs are gliding. I am on roller skates! I'm trying to not go too fast, but even without moving my feet, I keep going forward without effort.

The voices are swirling now, coming into my hearing, going out of my hearing. I am not recognizing the words. Why do I feel like they are talking about me? No one else is in the hallway.

Will I get in trouble for skating inside this place? Not if they can't catch me.

NICHOLAS
Now

As Nick approached the patient, he saw that same, familiar, beautiful face, but now very bruised and swollen. Her eyes were closed, and she was hooked up to an IV, but she was breathing on her own. She looked like she was in a deep sleep. He knew she would be happy to see him when she awakened. He had waited so long to see her again – he knew she had to feel the same way about him. She must have missed having him in her life as much as he had missed her all these years.

"Mandy," Nick said softly, expecting her to open her eyes. "I am so sorry. Not for this, well, yes, for this. I shouldn't have taken so long to respond to you. If I had answered your last letter that you sent me, none of this would have happened. Our lives would have taken a completely different direction, and we would have been together all this time." He leaned over her so he could look directly into her face. He was a tall man, which made it easy for him to stretch over the bed rails comfortably.

"But that doesn't matter now. Right now, finally, we are together, and we will be together for the rest of our lives. I am going to take you away from all this, to my house, to our home, a home I have been preparing just for us. Mandy, I need you. I need you so much. I have never known anyone else like you, and no one else can ever take your place in my heart." He looked for a sign that she could hear him, a flicker of her eye, or a twitch of her mouth. She seemed to be smiling, but, as he fondly recalled from grade school, her mouth naturally curved up at the edges of her lips, so she always looked like she was smiling. He gently took hold of her hand.

"Remember that song by the Moody Blues, the one that says, 'I know you're out there somewhere?' The first time I heard it, I felt they wrote it just for us. Every time I hear it, I think about you and I wonder where you are and what you are doing. You have always been in my heart. I have been waiting for the day when I would see you again. I knew this day would come – it had to. We were always meant to be together, even after all the mistakes I made that drove us apart.

"Now, finally, here we are together. You have no idea how much I have been missing you. I never want you to be hurting, not ever again. I never want us to be apart again, not ever."

A short, squat nurse came in the room to check Mandy's vital signs. Nick discreetly let go of Mandy's hand.

"How are you doing, young man?" the nurse asked, waddling around to the other side of the bed.

"Fine," he said, standing upright and stepping away from Mandy's side. He smiled, thinking that he was probably older than she was. Although he was a doctor and she was a nurse, he was still bashful in social situations. Since he no longer worked at this hospital, he felt as if he had no authority, no right to ask this nurse any questions about Mandy.

"And how is our patient?" she asked, writing notes on Mandy's chart.

"The same," he said, not offering a medical opinion, not wanting her to know he was a doctor. Women, especially nurses, made him very uncomfortable when they knew he was a doctor, as if that gave them a special connection to him.

He didn't want to be connected to any female but Mandy.

"Most patients eventually awaken from a coma," she said, presumably in an effort to encourage him.

Nick blinked and looked again at Mandy. She was in a coma? His colleague, Andrew, hadn't mentioned that fact. Nick began to look at his beloved in a different way. She was so vulnerable, totally unaware that she was completely dependent on the hospital staff to take care of her needs. He closely examined her face. She would eventually awaken; she had to come back to him.

"Are you a relative?" the nurse asked, checking the IV line that was connected to Mandy.

"No," he said, thinking that he hoped to be soon. He planned to soon be a very close relative, as soon as they could get married.

"Then I need to ask you to leave for a few minutes while I take care of some things for Amanda," she said, winking at him before going to the sink to wash her hands.

"Yes, of course," he said, not wanting to be in the same room with this nurse. He didn't like the way she said 'Amanda,' as if Mandy were in trouble in grade school. She didn't know Mandy at all, not like he knew her.

Nick left the room and headed for the hospital cafeteria. How long had it been since he had eaten, anyway? Not since before he had heard about the accident, which was yesterday – or was it the day before?

NICHOLAS
Then

"Class, today we're going to play dodge ball," Mrs. Graves told them, as they stepped out onto the playground. The crisp autumn day was sunny, and some of the girls were shivering with their bare legs beneath their dresses. "Has anyone played this before?"

"Yeah," Victor Booha said, always the one to speak up, always the one to draw attention to himself. "My brother plays it with me. He throws the ball at me and I catch it, and I throw it back at him. We get one point when we hit, and whoever gets to 10 points first is the winner. I can really smack him a good one!"

"This is something like that," Mrs. Graves said, holding the big red rubber ball, "but we have two teams. We take turns, one team at a time, throwing the ball, and the other team has to jump out of the way, dodge the ball. Each team is up three times, and each person gets one throw each time you are up. The team that hits the other team with the ball the most times is the winner.

"Today, since Marjorie is not here, we have 17 girls and 17 boys. Two even teams. We will play girls against boys. Now, the rule is, you have to throw the ball at the legs, not at the torso."

"What's a torso?" Tony Lagoni asked.

"The torso is the body," Mrs. Graves explained.

"Why didn't you just say the body?" Victor asked. "We know what a body is."

Several girls giggled. They giggled at everything Victor said. Nick noticed that Mandy was not giggling. His eyes were fixed on her. She stole glance at him, gave him the tiniest smile, making his heart race. Her cheeks turned bright red as she deliberately looked away from him.

"I wanted you to learn a new word," Mrs. Graves said sternly. "Now, the girls will throw first. Boys, you line up against the wall, over there, and girls, you line up on this line over here."

Nick didn't like this game, before they even started. He didn't want to throw a ball at a girl, not even at snotty Debbie Rosterson, who sat right behind him in class and was always telling him she wanted to kiss him. His grandparents had taught him to always respect girls, and never, never hit them or hurt them in any way.

He followed the boys as they lined up against the brick wall on the outside of the multi-purpose room. The sun, low on the horizon, was shining in their faces. Nick squinted, and he noticed that Mandy had moved to the end of the line, his end, so they were matched up with each other.

Mrs. Graves gave the ball to Janice Spender, the first girl in line. Janice took the ball doubtfully. Mrs. Graves blew the whistle, signaling the beginning of the game. Janice, a thin, frail girl, lifted the ball above her head and, with great effort, lobbed it toward the line of boys standing against the brick wall. The ball bounced in front of Mark Hammer, and Mark easily stepped out of the way and the ball bounced against the wall and rolled back to the line of girls. The boys all laughed – all except Nick.

"Good try, Janice," Mrs. Graves said. "Susan B., it's your turn. Oh, I forgot to mention, the team that is against the wall is not allowed to touch the ball. If you touch the ball with your hands, that is a point for the other team."

Susan picked up the ball and screwed up her face to put in her best effort. The ball slowly sailed toward Victor, who dramatically stepped sideways in slow motion.

"That's none for the girls!" Curtis Merlino shouted, as the ball hit the wall and bounced on the ground, back to the girls.

Terry Winters was up next. She was very athletic, a fast runner, and Nick thought she might have a chance to hit someone. She drew back the ball with one hand and fired it toward the line of boys at the wall, hitting Mark Hammer's shoe and bouncing off at a weird angle. The boys began to taunt him.

"Mark got hit by a girl!"

"She got you! You must love her!" The boys were roaring with laughter.

"Mark loves Terry!"

"Terry loves Mark!"

"Good one, Terry!" Mrs. Graves cheered. "That's one point for the girls!" She took out her clicker, the one she used to keep score, and clicked it one time.

The ball went back and forth, from the girls to the wall, with only one more girl hitting a boy with it, scoring just one more point, until it came to Mandy, the last one in line. She timidly held the ball. Nick could see that she was as uncomfortable with this game as he was.

"Come on, Mandy," Victor shouted. "We don't have all day!"

Mandy tossed the ball directly at Nick. Although the ball was moving slowly, he let it brush his pant leg, as he made an exaggerated effort to get out of the way.

"Nick got hit by a girl!" the taunting began.

"Nick loves Mandy!" Tom Brewster shouted.

"He really does! Look how red his face is!" Victor added.

Nick could feel that his face was on fire, and the mention of it just made it hotter.

"Okay, class, let's trade places," Mrs. Graves said in her outside voice. "Girls, line up against the wall."

"Terry, I'm gonna get you!" Mark shouted.

"Now, remember, boys, you can only hit their legs," Mrs. Graves warned.

Victor was first in line. He took the ball and made wild eyes at his line of targets. "Who wants to be first?" he yelled.

Not surprisingly, he didn't get a response. The girls were using their arms to try to shield themselves.

Victor gripped the rubber ball in one hand and fired it at the line of girls. His throw was too high – the ball hit Mandy squarely in the forehead, knocking her head against the brick wall. She lost her balance, stumbling against the wall, falling to her knees. Nick could see tears in her eyes as she stood up and brushed down her dress.

"Victor Edward!" Mrs. Graves shouted. She always used the first and middle name when she was really mad at a student. "You are out of the game! Go sit on the merry-go-round until the game is over!"

"Crybaby!" Victor shouted. "Mandy is just a crybaby! Boys, one, girls, three! Boys are gonna win!" he jeered, as he sauntered over to the merry-go-round.

"The rules are, no hitting above the waist!" Mrs. Graves reminded them loudly.

Next was Tom Brewster's turn. He was a big boy, but never wanted to break any rules. He grabbed the ball and threw it, not his hardest, but hard, at the girls as they stood against the wall, some of them covering their faces. The ball hit Susan B's thighs, just below her dress. She lost her balance, falling against the brick wall. Nick could see huge red marks appear immediately on her bare legs where the ball had hit. He hated this game already.

"Two-three!" Tom shouted triumphantly, as Susan B. rubbed her injured thighs.

"Terry, look out!" Mark shouted, as he slammed the ball at her, just missing her face. She hit her head against the wall as she dodged the ball.

"Missed!" Terry shouted, although she was still injured.

As the ball was thrown, nearly every boy hit a girl on her bare legs, making that awful smacking sound as it hit. Nick felt so sorry for the girls. Even the ones who could dodge the ball couldn't dodge the wall. When it was Merle Comcleen's turn, he also hit Mandy, this time in the legs. She was thrust against the wall, hitting her head again, trying unsuccessfully not to cry. She looked down at her hand that had broken her fall, and Nick could see that it was bleeding.

The ball was passed to Nick. The girls, several of them crying, and many with red welts on their thighs, looked at him with fear. He began to draw it back, but he couldn't do it. This game was against everything he had been taught. He couldn't hit a girl, even with a big red rubber ball. He tossed the ball so it bounced halfway between the two lines of players.

"Oh, come on," Mark said. "You're not even trying! You can throw harder than that!"

Nick shook his head. "We are already up 13 to 3," he said.

"Okay, girls, your turn to throw," Mrs. Graves said, as the teams traded places.

"Mrs. Graves, can I go to the nurse?" Mandy asked softly. She lifted her bleeding hand.

"Oh, that's just a scrape, Amanda," Mrs. Graves said. "Wipe those pebbles out of it. I can give you a Band-Aid when we get back to the classroom. Now, get over there! It's your team's chance to catch up!"

The second round of the game was even more pathetic than the first, since most of the girls were now hurt. They threw the ball like, well, girls, and didn't score another point in the second round, as the ball bounced in front the boys and they had time to step out of the way. When the girls were again against the wall, the boys showed no mercy, smacking them mostly on the legs, but a few on the face or chest. The boys who broke the rules were removed from the game, but the damage had been done. By the third round, only 11 boys were left, and six of them took advantage of knowing this was their last chance in this game to hit a girl as hard as he could. They didn't care if they had to join Victor on the merry-go-round.

When the game was over, final score 36-4, nearly all the girls were crying. Except for Terry, who was wearing leotards, all the girls had red ball-marks/welts on their legs, and five of them had been hit in the head by the ball. Most of the girls had hit their heads at least once against the brick wall, and they looked stunned, stumbling and falling against each other as they returned to the classroom. Mandy trailed behind the other girls, with no one to lean on. She kept her eyes on her bleeding hands as she brushed little pieces of gravel out of the scrapes she had received during the game.

Nick longed to put his arm around Mandy and comfort her – she had been hit six times and looked utterly defeated – but he couldn't do it. He couldn't risk the ridicule from the other boys.

This was one game he would not be able to discuss at the dinner table with his grandparents.

MANDY

I am in the marketplace, trying to locate fresh mangoes. Every other kind of fruit and vegetable is on display, but no mangoes. The market is crowded with people, too many people, and I wish I had just gone to Fred Meyer for my shopping, where there is lots of space and few people, or at least, not a pushing, shoving mob.

My feet are tired, and my arm is hurting. I can't recall why. I am usually in such good physical condition. I have to be, for my family. They need me to be well all the time.

Where is my family? We came here together. I see Greg Harper, an old boyfriend of mine. What is he doing here? I haven't seen him since college, but he is approaching me like he still knows me.

"Come on, let's go home," he says, grabbing my sore arm.

"Ow!" I say. "My arm hurts!" I try to pull it away from him, wishing I could yank it from his grip, but it has no strength, just pain.

"Let's get out of here," he insists, pulling me, again, my sore arm.

I shake my head, wincing with pain. I don't belong with him anymore. We broke up years ago, but he is here with me, acting like he owns me. That was one of the reasons I broke up with him.

"No," I say, still shaking my head.

I know I don't belong to Greg. No, I have a husband, but he doesn't own me. He loves me! We have been married for a long time, happily married. I can't remember who he is! What does he look like? I know he is handsome, and he is very nice. I know I am not with Greg anymore! Who is my husband? I have to find him. Who is he?

This is like a bad dream. Maybe it is a dream! I certainly hope so.

NICHOLAS
Now

Nick figured the man who so quickly skedaddled out of Mandy's room must have been an orderly. He probably noticed how beautiful she was and wanted to spend a few minutes with her. No matter, he was gone. Nick shot a glance up and down the hall and didn't see anyone else coming towards the room as he stepped inside, close to Mandy.

She was still the most beautiful girl in the world, even with the swollen face and bruises. He had waited so long for this moment, this turn of circumstances that brought them back together. He had so much to tell her, and now she had all the time in the world, so to speak.

"Hey, Mandy, I'm back. This time, I'm not going anywhere. I'm not moving to Montana or to Boston. I'm not going anywhere without you."

He paused to see if perhaps she would react in some way, but she just stayed still with her permanent smile on her lips. He leaned in closer, to be sure she could hear him.

"I know I messed up when we were in the sixth grade, when I told those guys I didn't like you. Didn't you know I didn't mean it? I didn't know you were listening. Then I saw your face and I knew you heard me, and I really hurt you. I kept thinking I would have a chance to make it up to you, and I would tell you the truth. I realize now, those three times you came to our house, you were giving me another opportunity, but someone else was always there. One time it was my grandma, one time it was Brian Mummy, and the other time it was my grandma and my grandpa. I had to talk to you in private, but we never had another chance to be alone together. Now I know, I should have shared my feelings with you then. My mistake in the sixth grade separated us and ruined my whole life – until now, that is.

"You have to know how much I need you. I have always needed you. You were the one – you ARE the only one who can make my life complete. I need you, Mandy."

NICHOLAS
Then

"All right, class," Mrs. Graves said, "single file, and let us walk quietly down the hall to the multi-purpose room."

Nick put his paper and pencil inside his desk quickly so he could catch up with Mandy. He was so happy things were working out for him. Today was the school Christmas program, and he had managed to get a place right beside Mandy while they sang. This meant they had to sit next to each other during the entire program. During all six rehearsals they had been together, and Mrs. Graves had decided they should stand by each other since they were both about the same height. Mandy was tall, for a girl. He thought Mrs. Graves knew that they liked each other, and she must have felt a little generous toward them, maybe because it was the Christmas season.

Mandy was waiting for him in the hallway.

"Are you waiting for your *boy*-friend?" Victor teased, laughing, as he leaned his head right into her face.

Nick saw Mandy blush. She didn't answer Victor. They all knew students weren't allowed to talk in the hallway, but he kind of wished she would have told Victor, yes, she was waiting for Nick, her boyfriend. He wanted to hear her say it, now that it was sort of official.

Their class was the first to arrive in the multi-purpose room. The students took their seats. Nick was happy that he was sitting beside Mandy, but he was not happy with the song their class would be singing: 'Away in a Manger.' It seemed like a little kid song, not a song for second graders to be singing. Many of the boys had already voiced their protests, but Mrs. Graves had selected the song, and that was final. The other class of second graders, Miss Kennedy's class, would get to sing a better song than theirs. Then both classes would sing 'Silent Night' together, and at the end of the program, the entire school would stand on the steps in front of the stage to sing 'O Come, All Ye Faithful,' and 'Joy to the World.'

Nick wanted to talk to Mandy as the other classes filed silently into their designated places, but this was not a time when they could be talking. The parents – and in his case, grandparents – were seated in folding chairs in the middle of the multi-purpose room facing the stage, while the classes, from kindergarten to sixth grade, were seated on the floor, in order, on both sides of the multi-purpose room, facing each other. The kindergarten teacher stood in front of her class, made a motion with her arms for the students to stand, and the little kids stood up and walked very neatly and got onto the first two steps in front of the stage. It looked to Nick like only the afternoon kindergarten kids were there, since there were only about fifteen little kids there.

The teacher raised her arms and the kids began to sing-shout 'Rudolph, the Red-nosed Reindeer.' When they finished the song, one tiny boy took a bow, and the audience laughed as they applauded.

As the kindergartners took their seats, the first graders got in place on the steps in front of the stage. The first-grade classes were completely full, with thirty-six students in each of the two classes, and they were kind of remarkable in that they had five sets of identical twins in that grade, three sets of girls and two sets of boys, while there were no other sets of twins in the rest of the school. As expected, all the students were dressed in their Sunday best for the Christmas Program, and each set of twins was dressed exactly alike, in case someone might not know they were twins.

The first graders sang 'The Friendly Beasts,' with a few students making different animal noises, drawing smiles and laughter from the parents. They followed with 'Up on the Housetop,' with all the hand motions, including snapping their fingers for the click-click-clicks and folding their hands across their bellies and leaning back for the ho-ho-hos. The audience loved them and applauded loudly for them.

Mrs. Graves' second grade class was up next. Nick made sure he bumped (gently) into Mandy at least twice while they were taking their place on the stage steps. Since they were in the back row, Mandy was the only one who knew of his little shenanigans. She was smiling broadly as they sang their song, a song that should have been sung by preschoolers. Nick knew he wasn't imagining that the applause they received was much more subdued than had been for the previous classes. The parents were probably wondering why these mature second graders were singing such a baby song.

They left the stage steps and Miss Kennedy's second grade class replaced them. Their song was 'O Christmas Tree,' and when they began singing a verse in German, the parents were clearly impressed, and they applauded enthusiastically. Nick couldn't see his grandparents from where he was sitting, but he knew they were there. He hoped they weren't embarrassed by the baby song his class was forced to sing. He scanned the audience and wondered who Mandy's parents were. He couldn't tell by looking.

The third grade class sang 'The Twelve Days of Christmas' with groups of students singing about each day, the whole class loudly singing the twelfth day together. The audience loved them. Next, the fourth graders sang a very joyful rendition of 'Jingle Bells' and 'Silver Bells.' Some lucky students got to shake ribbons of bells and didn't have to actually sing.

The fifth and sixth graders took the stage together, completely filling the steps in front of the stage. Two rows of students stood in front of the steps, and one row stood on the stage, making quite an impressive choir. One of the sixth grade teachers, Mrs. Metcalf, stood in front of them. She raised her arms and a group of girls only began to sing 'O Little Town of Bethlehem.' When they finished the first verse, boys began to sing the second verse. Mrs. Metcalf was directing them so fiercely, so passionately, as they went directly into 'Hark the Herald Angels Sing,' and the different levels of voices blended so beautifully. The audience began to applaud; but their applause was cut short when the most glorious sounds came from the choir as they sang 'Angels We Have Heard on High.' They were especially impressive during the gloooooooooria part, when all the high and low voices seemed to chase each other, following the lead of their director. When the song was finished, they received a standing ovation. Nick stole a glance at Mandy. Her face was lit up brighter than a Christmas tree. She was entranced by the beautiful sound of the choir.

As the rest of the classes stood in place to join for the final songs, Mandy leaned over and whispered to Nick, "I can't wait until we get to sixth grade and sing that song, with Mrs. Metcalf directing."

"Me, too," Nick whispered, although he didn't really care if he ever sang that song. He just wanted to be doing what Mandy was doing, and he liked that she was planning for them that far ahead.

MANDY

All afternoon I have been in the kitchen baking Christmas cookies. Every year we have so many Christmas traditions that we follow. We, our family, as well as our church family, are satisfied to know what is going to happen, the same way it always does at this time of year. We will be taking some of these cookies to the nursing home tonight when we go caroling. I love to see the faces of the residents light up when they see us, and especially when they see the children's choir singing with us.

I make note of where I stored the Christmas song books last year, and the Christmas hats we wear when we go caroling. Christmas music is playing on the stereo, giving that holiday spirit to our entire house, along with the scents of gingerbread and cinnamon.

Caleb and Joshua come bursting in from the cold.

"Can we have a cookie?" Caleb asks. I am the only one who can tell our twins apart. Even their father gets them mixed up. He calls both of them 'my number one son. I usually give him a clue, such as 'Caleb is wearing his red shirt today,' or 'Joshua didn't comb his hair this morning.'

"Just one," I say, knowing one will lead to another, but I have to start somewhere, at a very low number because starting with two would lead to two at a time. Caleb grabs the biggest one he sees, a fat Christmas tree, but Joshua examines them to find just the one he wants. I am so thankful to have these two boys, and I smile to myself as I think about later tonight when we will tell them they will be getting a new brother or sister next year.

The cookies look good and I am tempted to eat one also, but I know I need to avoid the sugar. I have already gained too much weight and am only in my third month of pregnancy. My hand goes to one of the Santa Claus cookies with pink frosting – it didn't turn out as red as it should have – and I put it in my mouth. Funny, it has no taste.

I look at my boys and they seem to be shorter than they really are. They have grown so much this year. I put one hand on each of their heads and as I slowly pull them up, my boys grow taller, to the true height that they are now.

I go into the bathroom and look at myself in the mirror. I see the reflection of someone else, a lady that is not even looking at me.

That is how I know this is a dream.

JAMIE
Now

As fate would have it, she was again in room 304. Fate, at last, was in control. Jamie wanted to say he was lucky this time, although he had never before been lucky. No, he couldn't say lucky, because Amanda, again, was in the hospital with serious injuries. The newspaper had said her husband and two children had died in the car accident and she was seriously injured with a possible concussion. Some people might say she was lucky to be alive, but Jamie knew fate was finally bringing them together, bringing her to him, after all these years. Throughout the other lifetimes he had lived without her, he had always kept in the back of his mind that they were meant to be together; she was the girl for him; fate had to finally bring them back to the same course – and now, here they were.

He paced the small waiting area, wondering when he would be able to see her. A doctor moved by swiftly, as if trying to avoid conversation, and Jamie wondered if he knew anything about Amanda.

Yet, how could the doctor know anything about Amanda, other than her current condition? Jamie knew her. He had known her for so long. He knew her so well. He was the one who knew her favorite color – turquoise – and that she had always loved cats and the smell of lilacs. She was brave around her friends but shy around other people. She was smart: smart enough to get straight A's in school and go to college. She always noticed every detail and she was great at telling stories. And she always included all the details. She quickly memorized the names of everyone in her classes and she always knew what was on the lunch menu for the entire week.

The only thing she had ever overlooked were his feelings for her. She treated him like he was her very best friend, but she never did notice how much he loved her. He had never told her – not yet.

JAMIE
Then

As Jamie was riding his bike to school on the first day of 7th grade, he tried to not think about all the new kids he would meet. Four elementary schools came together in this one junior high, so many new kids in one place. In six years at Lincoln Elementary, he had finally become comfortable with his classmates; maybe not enough to initiate a conversation with anyone but his best friend, Jerry, but enough to answer in class when a teacher called on him. The kids had finally stopped picking on him. His shyness kept him from participating in many activities, and his family was always otherwise occupied, so he was glad he had his bike, his constant companion. His dad had even bought him a new Schwinn 10-speed for the school year, which he was riding now, down Chestnut Avenue to 40th Avenue.

As he waited for the traffic to pass so he could make a left turn onto 40th, a girl on a yellow 10-speed went flying down 40th, just behind the cars. He quickly pedaled across the street and nearly caught up with her, following in the lane behind her, all the way to Wilson Junior High School. Maybe she was new at this school too – maybe they would have some classes together. As she slowed her bike to turn into the bike parking area, he admired her long brown hair as it drifted behind her, settling onto her back as she stopped. He wanted to speak to her, but instead he hid behind the mop of hair that nearly covered his eyes. He moved to the far end of the bike racks.

"Hey, we have the same bike!" she exclaimed, speaking to him, breathing heavily from her ride. "Except yours is brown. But they are just the same!"

"Yeah," was all he could muster, noticing that her yellow Schwinn was indeed the same model as his brown one.

"Aren't you going to lock it up?" she asked, undoing her lock, which was coiled around her seat post.

He never locked his bike. When his last one was stolen, his dad just bought him a new one. His brand-new lock was at home.

"I don't have a lock," he said, which wasn't exactly a lie. He didn't have a lock with him.

"Well, you don't want someone to steal your bike," she told him. "Bring it over here. We can lock ours together."

He couldn't believe his luck! This cute girl was asking him to lock his bike together with hers! He walked his bike over so it was right beside hers.

"I'm Amanda," she said, weaving her bike lock through his and her bikes and the rack.

"Jamie," he managed to say.

"You know, you can't leave until I do," she said, snapping her lock shut and twirling the dial, "unless you leave your bike here."

"I won't," he said quietly. He didn't know if she even heard him.

"Are you starting 7th grade today?" she asked, gathering up her things from the small pouch that was attached to the back of her seat.

He nodded. How could he talk to a cute girl like this? She was looking right at him!

"Me, too," she confirmed. "Who do you have for homeroom?"

"I dunno," he mumbled, pulling his schedule from his pocket. He hadn't thought where he would go, beyond the bike racks.

"I have Mr. Arthur for Art," she said, as if she had already memorized her schedule before the first class even started. "Mr. Art for Art! Ha-ha!"

He looked at his schedule, so complicated, with alternating third periods and a rotating 7th period. He had nine classes on his schedule, but only six of them met each day. Why couldn't they just have one class with one teacher, like they did in elementary school, so he would know where to go, and he didn't have to be around so many new people in one day? And how could he even know where he was supposed to be, with all these alternations and rotations?

"I have him, too," he said, when he finally located his first period class on the schedule.

"I'm so glad!" Amanda said. "None of my other friends have him first period. That means you and I will start with the same class, together, every day!"

She mentioned 'other friends.' Was she implying that he was one of her friends already? He smiled shyly, not knowing what to say. He just nodded, not meeting her eyes.

"Do you know where room 304 is?" she asked.

Jamie shook his head.

"Let's go find it together," she said.

He couldn't have said it any better.

MANDY

I have a long way to go before I get home. I am just to Union Gap, so I am within walking distance – if walking distance is more than a few miles. I know how to get there, even if I am not in a familiar neighborhood. As long as I keep that brown hill within my sight, behind me and to my left, I am on the right route to get home. Most of the way will be flat until the final mile or so, as I gradually make my way up hill. Then I will get to the dip on North 48th, where the road goes down and then it goes all the way up to Scenic Drive. Thankfully, I won't have to go to the top of the hill. Our street is about halfway up, a climb that gets my heart beating and makes my breath short, but I have been making the climb since I was 6 years old, when we moved to that neighborhood.

I think about calling my parents to come and pick me up, to give me a ride the rest of the way home, but I want to surprise them. They don't know I'm coming, and won't they be happy to see me when I walk up the street and open the front door? I can imagine them now, coming to greet me, my mom throwing her arms around me and my dad standing slightly behind her, with that delightfully surprised smile and that look that tells me that he is proud of me. They are going to be so surprised! I can't wait to see them! I miss them so much.

My legs have been walking for so long, I can't really feel them. They are not tired, they are not aching, which doesn't make sense, considering the miles they have already brought me. Home is within reach! I am going to make it soon, before dark. I don't recognize this area at all, so I just keep moving in the right direction, knowing this journey will, at last, eventually, come to an end. My heart leaps with that awareness.

Nobody is outside, on the streets or in the yards, and I suddenly get the feeling that I am running out of time. I am so much closer to my goal than I have ever been; I have to make it! As the world around me begins to get hazy, as if it will dissolve before I can get home, a portion of a poem comes to mind, and I smile to myself. I have miles to go before I wake... miles to go, before I wake.

NICHOLAS
Then

Nick fidgeted in his seat. He didn't like the new arrangement their fourth-grade teacher, Mrs. Mattson, had set for their desks. Before, he was always near the back of the room, on the far side of the room, away from the hall door and in the second row from the windows, since they were seated alphabetically, and his last name started with an R. Mandy always ended up near the front of the room, in the second row from the door, since her last name started with an F. With that arrangement, he was able to stare at her any time they weren't reading their textbooks, any time the teacher or anyone else was talking, without looking like he was staring at her. He could also slip her a note any time he needed to leave the classroom, since he had to walk right by her desk. Now that they were seated reversed alphabetically, they had exchanged seats. Mandy now sat where he used to sit, and he was in her old desk, right in front of the class, directly in front of Mrs. Mattson's desk. He couldn't look at Mandy without everyone seeing him, so he had to sneak a glance whenever he got something out of his desk, or accidentally on purpose dropped his pencil on the floor.

He opened his desk to remove his science book and took a quick glance at Mandy, who was doing the same thing. Before he closed his desk, he noticed something faintly carved in the wood, on the underside of his desktop. 'MF + NR' was carved inside a tiny heart. Nick ran his finger over it, to feel the texture, and before he closed his desk, he looked quickly back at Mandy again. She was looking right at him, smiling.

He felt himself blush. His desktop slipped from his hands and it slammed shut, making a loud bang.

"Nicholas!" Mrs. Mattson said. "Please don't slam your desk shut!"

"I'm sorry," he said. "It slipped out of my hand." He was so embarrassed, all the kids in the class were laughing at him. He could feel his face growing redder and redder, so he stuck it in his science book to wait for the laughter to subside.

"Class, before we start with our science lesson, I have an announcement to make," Mrs. Mattson said. Nick could hear the sounds of his classmates silencing as their teacher waited for their full attention. He continued to stare into his book, sure that his face was still red.

"We are going to do an operetta," she said, as if this were of some great importance to fourth graders.

"What's an operetta?" Tony Lagoni asked.

"An operetta is like a little opera," Mrs. Mattson explained.

"What's an opera?" Tony asked. A few kids chuckled, but Nick was sure no one in class really knew what an opera was.

"An opera is like a musical play," Mrs. Mattson said. "We will have dancing and singing, and we will invite all of your parents to come and watch, after we learn our parts and rehearse."

A couple of cheers and many groans filled the classroom.

"Don't worry, everyone will have a part," their teacher assured her students.

"So, what's the play we're going to do?" Heidi Shrimpkin asked.

"The operetta we will be doing is 'Cinderella,'" Mrs. Mattson said proudly.

"That's a girl program!" Victor complained. "That's for sissies!"

An extremely loud cheer came across the hall from the other fourth grade class, Mrs. Pott's class. Nick joined the rest of his class in turning towards the door to see what the cause of the excitement might be.

"Mrs. Pott must have told them the name of the play they are going to be doing this spring," Mrs. Mattson said.

"I bet it won't be 'Snow White' or any other girly program," Tom Brewster said.

"Mrs. Pott has decided they will be doing 'Treasure Island,'" Mrs. Mattson said, "but they won't get to do the singing and dancing, because they are just doing a play, not an operetta."

"They are doing 'Treasure Island?'" Tom asked. "That's my favorite book!"

"I hate singing and dancing! Can I transfer to Mrs. Pott's class?" Mark Hammer asked.

"Me, too!" Brian Mummy shouted. "I don't want to do any girly dancing and singing!"

"Me neither!" Tony added.

Everyone in class started talking at the same time, mostly complaining about 'Cinderella' and begging for 'Treasure Island.' Mrs. Mattson settled the noise by banging her pointing stick on the chalkboard.

"Quiet, class!" she said sternly. "Mrs. Pott's class is doing the play 'Treasure Island,' and we are doing 'Cinderella' as an operetta. You can be thankful that you won't have any lines to learn like the other class will. We will have seven songs to learn, and, with the exception of one song, which three boys will sing, the whole class will sing together. This is going to be an experience you will remember for the rest of your lives."

"Do we have to try out for the parts?" Marsha McCormick asked. "I have been the lead ballerina in my ballet class for two months, so I should get to be Cinderella."

"You are not going to try out for the parts," Mrs. Mattson said. "No one is going to audition. I have already selected your parts, according to your academic standing. Those of you with higher grades will get the lead parts."

"When do we start?" Michael Barron asked. "I better start getting down there."

The students snickered at his remark.

"Don't worry, Michael, you won't be getting one of the lead parts," Mrs. Mattson said. "We have twelve lead parts, for the top twelve students, six girls and six boys, and the rest of the class will be dancers at the ball. And you will all get to sing."

The boys groaned loudly.

"Now, I have already chosen the cast members," Mrs. Mattson continued, dismissing the resistance of the class.

Everyone knew that Mandy was the smartest student in the class. She was the farthest ahead in the self-paced reading program by five colors, she had already finished all the pre-algebra math quizzes, she had turned in twice as many book reports as anyone else in the class, which were represented by cars of a train going around the classroom, and she had finished and turned in all of the social studies homework for the rest of the year. Nick knew she would be chosen to be Cinderella. Nick was so proud of her.

He wondered who would get to be her prince: Tom, Brian,

or him. They were the three boys who were always in competition to be at the top of the class. He had to be the prince, the one who would get to dance with Mandy, to hold her and look into her eyes while they danced, and possibly get to kiss her at the end of the operetta. The room was completely quiet as all the students looked at Mrs. Mattson expectantly. She pulled a sheet of paper out of her desk.

"Now, for Cinderella, we have to make an exception," Mrs. Mattson said, looking around the room before she began reading the list of cast members. "We all know that Amanda is the top student in the class."

Nick shot a quick glance in Mandy's direction. She was blushing, looking down at her desk.

"However," Mrs. Mattson continued, "Amanda has short, curly, brown hair. Cinderella has to have long, flowing, blond hair."

"The Cinderella on TV had brown hair," Terry said, in Mandy's defense.

"We need a Cinderella with long, blond, flowing hair," Mrs. Mattson said firmly.

"It's not Rapunzel!" Terry shouted. "It's Cinderella, and there's nothing that says she has to have long hair. Mandy should have the lead role, since she is the top student in this class."

"The decision has already been made," Mrs. Mattson snapped. "Janice is the third highest girl in the class, and she has long, blond hair. Janice will play Cinderella in our operetta." Mrs. Mattson raised her head slightly and looked down her nose at the class, signifying that there would be no further discussion.

"Thank you, Mrs. Mattson," Janice said softly.

Nick was furious. Janice was a nice girl, but this was

not fair to Mandy. He turned to catch a glimpse of Mandy and saw that she was looking away from the teacher, out the window. He could just barely see her reflection in the window – she was crying. He could feel his heart pounding in his chest. Since she was not going to be Cinderella, he certainly was not going to be the prince. Any other boy could be Janice's prince.

Mrs. Mattson wrote the names of the roles on the chalkboard: Cinderella; the Wicked Stepmother; the stepsisters, Prunella, Druscilla, Esmerelda; the Fairy Godmother; the Prince; the King; the Prince's Assistant; and the three messengers of the king.

"Since Mandy is the top student in the class, we can't have her be the Wicked Stepmother or one of the three Wicked Stepsisters," Mrs. Mattson said, slowly shaking her head.

Nick glanced back at Mandy again and saw that she had put her head down on her arms on her desk, hiding her face. He wished he could do something to make her feel better.

"Roberta, you will be the Wicked Stepmother," Mrs. Mattson said. The class was completely quiet, and Nick had a feeling it had something to do with the fact that Roberta had a very large nose. "Kathy, Kim and Lori, you will be Prunella, Druscilla and Esmerelda, the wicked stepsisters. Sally, since you are the tallest girl in the class, you will be the Fairy Godmother. I already have a dress for you, and it is very long. It should fit you perfectly. Tony, Tom and Brian, you will be the messengers of the king. You will get to sing a song by yourselves, well, together, but just the three of you. Mark, you will be the prince's assistant. You will be the one who gets to put the glass slipper on all the girls. Jay, you will be the King, the father of the Prince."

Mrs. Mattson stopped talking and began writing the

names of the cast members next to their roles on the chalk-board. The class was silent as she skipped over the role of the Prince and filled in all the other names. When she was finished writing all of the names but the Prince's, she placed the piece of chalk in the chalk tray.

"So, who gets to be the Prince?" Victor asked. He was unofficially known as Janice's boyfriend.

"Not you!" Mark said. "You are the opposite of the top boy student in this class!"

His remark triggered laughter in the class.

"It has to be Nick!" Roger Stempler stated. "Nick is the only one at the top of the class who doesn't have a role!"

"Nick plus Janice!" Mark said. "Nick is going to be Janice's prince!"

"You better not be!" Victor shouted, slapping his desk. "You better stay away from her, Robbins!"

Nick felt the back of his neck heating up. He was so embarrassed, and Mrs. Mattson hadn't said he was going to be the Prince. He glanced back at Mandy again and saw that she still had her head down, not participating in this class discussion. He looked over at Mrs. Mattson and saw that she was staring right at him, giving him the same look that Dr. Hoffman often gave Barnabas in 'Dark Shadows,' a look that said he should know what she was thinking.

"I don't want her!" Nick said, feeling his face getting so hot, it had to be sticking out at least two inches.

"Nicholas, you will be our Prince," Mrs. Mattson said firmly. She turned to the chalk board, picked up the piece of chalk and wrote Nick's name next to the word 'Prince.'

"I–" he began to protest, but realized it was worthless. As Mrs. Mattson had said, the decision had already been made. He was a bit flattered that he was chosen to be the

Prince, but he didn't want to dance with Janice. Sure, she was pretty, but she was not Mandy. He wanted to be Mandy's prince.

"Nicholas and Janice, I will need you to stay after school for a few minutes today," Mrs. Mattson instructed. "Also, I have permission slips for each of you that you will need your parents to sign before you can be in the operetta."

"My mom can't sign it," Jay announced. "She is on vacation for a few months. I guess I can't be in the operetta. Maybe you need to transfer me into Mrs. Pott's class."

"Jay, you know I live just down the street from you," Mrs. Mattson said, tapping her pointer on his desk. "I see your parents all the time. If you can't get your mom or dad to sign the permission slip, I will be happy to talk to them."

"Oh, I just remembered," Jay said, "Mom is back from vacation. She's coming back today!"

The class roared.

"During our physical education time today, we will go to the multi-purpose room and begin to learn our dance steps," Mrs. Mattson said. "This will be easy for most of you, because for the operetta, we will be dancing the glow-worm dance, the one we learned last month. As a matter of fact, in the spirit of the theater, let's skip our science lesson today and go to the multi-purpose room right now. We can get a head start on the dance. We only have two months to get everything right, oh, and you will each need to provide your own costumes. We can talk about that later. Spit-spot! Let's get moving!"

The class went, mostly unenthusiastically, to the multi-purpose room. The kitchen workers were just finishing putting away the lunch carts as the students filed into the large room.

"Okay, we will have two dance circles," Mrs. Mattson said, "one for the main dancers and the other for the rest of the class. Class members, you who are not part of the cast, when you are not dancing, you will be in the choir. You will be on those bleachers over there. During the ball, you will come and dance down here, in front of the stage. The main cast members will dance up on the stage. You will have to be careful while doing the glow-worm dance, because of the steps. When you come around the front of the stage, since it is so small, you will have to dance down the steps backwards, and then dance back up the steps. The rest of the class, you will do the glow-worm dance down here.

"We can't practice on the stage right now, because the sports equipment is being stored up there now, but we will get that moved soon. Let's just practice both circles in front of the stage now, small circle, over here, large circle, over there."

Nick saw Mandy bravely joining the non-cast circle of dancers as Mrs. Mattson was matching up the cast dancers.

"Nick, you stand by Janice," she instructed. "Tony, Tom and Brian, you, the messengers of the king, will dance with the three wicked step sisters, Kathy and Kim and Lori. Mark, you will dance with Roberta. Oh, dear, we don't have anyone to dance with the King. Let's see, we need a Queen to dance with Jay."

Mrs. Mattson looked over at the non-cast group. Some of the girls were gathered in a group, chattering, not paying any attention to their teacher. Mandy stood alone, in the circle, but not with anyone else.

"Amanda, you can be the Queen. Come over here so you can dance with the King."

Nick saw Mandy's face light up as she became one of the chosen students. She scurried over to the smaller circle of

43

students to take her place beside Jay, the King. Nick smiled at her on the sly, so no one else would see it but her. Even though she had been his girlfriend for more than two years, proper protocol in the fourth grade did not allow them to be seen in public together, and their personal lives did not allow them to be alone together. They had an understanding that they were boyfriend and girlfriend, and the rest of the students knew it, too. Even the teachers were aware that they liked each other. More than anything, they held each other in their hearts.

As she passed by Nick, he whispered in her ear, "I guess you are now my mother."

Mandy's eyes sparkled as she giggled.

NICHOLAS
Now

Nick returned to Mandy's room with a full stomach. He hadn't noticed he was hungry, but when he smelled the food in the cafeteria, he realized he had been just about starving. The sub sandwich and bowl of vegetable beef soup really hit the spot, and he felt refreshed as well as rejuvenated.

He peeked into her room, relieved to see that no one else was in there with her. He briefly thought about her parents, who should be here, who would be here with her if they could. They had been killed in a car accident a few years ago. She didn't have any brothers or sisters. Mandy was an only child, as he was.

He quietly came into the room, standing close to Mandy. She hadn't moved one bit since he left. He wanted to tell her everything, now that they finally had this time together, with no one else to interrupt or distract or send either of them on another course. She had been in his heart for so long. He ached as he looked at her, thinking of the lost years they could have spent with each other. Yet, now those years were gone, smashed into a glob of memories, and they could start again, this time, as a couple.

"Mandy, I know you can hear me. You have no idea how much I have missed you. You do know I have always wanted to be with you," he said, leaning over her, looking into her face. "Ever since we met, I knew we were destined to be together, the same way my grandparents were, from a young age. I am so sorry I let you get away from me.

"I tried to have a good marriage," he said, settling into a chair beside Mandy's bed. He gently touched her hair, smoothing it back, away from her face. "It just didn't work for us because she wasn't you. It wasn't her fault. She was a good wife and she is a good mother. She just wasn't right for me. She just isn't you."

He put his hand on her arm, taking note of how dry her skin was. He looked at her hand as he spoke to her. "Everything she did, I subconsciously compared it to how I thought you would do it. I know now, I was trying to keep a door open for you to come back into my life. My heart was not ever with her, not completely, because I truly love you. I think I was just waiting with her until something better came along... someone better, and that someone was you.

"We stayed together for fourteen years, and we have two beautiful daughters, Angela and Aubrey, and I am ashamed to admit how often I secretly wished our girls were your daughters. I wanted them to look like you and to act like you, but how could they? You are not their mother. They turned out to be a lot like me, and I have a feeling they could see right through my act. I mean, they knew that I loved them, but both, especially Aubrey, who is so sensitive, well, I am afraid I made them feel like they weren't good enough, like I was expecting more from them than they could ever possibly give me, or more than they could possibly be to me.

"My wife and I separated years ago, and I moved as far away from her as I possibly could, here, to Seattle. I worked in this very hospital. You do know you are in a hospital, don't you? You can hear me, can't you, Mandy? Mandy, I need you to wake up and come back to me."

He gently rubbed her arm. He wanted to shake her awake, but he knew he couldn't do that – that was not the way to bring a person out of a coma.

He had time, now, if nothing else. He had Mandy now. He could wait. He had been waiting for this day for all those years. A little while longer would be no time at all. Now, finally, they were together for good.

MANDY

I climb up the bleachers to watch the football game, balancing my popcorn and a drink as I stretch my legs up the big steps. As I am looking for a seat, I see Nick sitting by himself. He pats the seat beside him, putting down a blanket for me. I am happy to see him. Where has he been all this time? Well, he is here now. I feel pleasantly surprised and relieved.

I struggle to sit without spilling anything, then I set my things beside me on the bench.

"What's the score?" I ask, looking down to the field.

"I'm not watching," he says. I feel his gaze is on me. "It is just a game."

I turn my head, wondering what he means by that. This is not just a game. We are here, but he has been gone for a long time. I haven't seen him in years, and now he is right here.

"I have two daughters," he says.

"I have twin sons," I tell him, then I wonder where they are. Why am I here without my sons? I begin to search the crowd, but too many people are blocking my view.

"I have been waiting for this moment, ever since our last kiss," Nick says softly.

The team must have scored a touchdown, since the crowd goes wild, yelling and cheering.

Nick moves closer to me, to kiss me, but I pull away from him. He is not the man I should be kissing right now.

NICHOLAS
Then

Three days before the operetta of 'Cinderella' was scheduled to be performed by Mrs. Mattson's fourth grade class at Gilbert Elementary School, Nick awakened not feeling well. He went into the kitchen where his grandmother was preparing breakfast. He smelled the coffee and bacon and wished he were feeling better. He doubted that he would be able to eat anything this morning.

"Grandma, I don't feel so good," he said, sliding into his chair at the small table.

His grandfather came into the kitchen. "You are just nervous about the play," he said, taking his seat.

"Don't worry, you will be fine," his grandmother said, putting plates of bacon and eggs and toast in front of Nick and his grandfather.

"It's not a play," Nick reminded them for the umpteenth time. "It's an operetta."

"An operetta," his grandmother repeated, bringing her own plate to the table and sitting with Nick and his grandfather.

"It's all the same to me," his grandfather said. "And apparently, it's the same to you, too, otherwise you wouldn't be so nervous that you are sick to your stomach. You obviously have stage fright."

"No, it's not my stomach," Nick said.

"You don't feel like you have a fever," his grandmother said, placing her wrist on his forehead. "You'll feel better when you get to school."

Nick took a few bites, but he couldn't eat any more. Maybe they were right, and he did have a case of stage fright.

"It's a nice, warm, spring day," his grandmother said. "Get your sweater. You don't need to wear your heavy coat today. Oh, here's your lunch." She handed him a brown bag that he knew held a tuna sandwich, a few potato chips in a plastic baggie, a small apple and a chocolate chip cookie. His grandfather handed him a nickel to buy his milk.

"Bye, Grandma, bye, Grandpa," he said, as he went out the front door. He walked the half block to school, grateful that the walk wasn't any longer, since he didn't have much energy.

By the time he got to the classroom, he was very hot. He was sure he had a fever by now, but, then, what did stage fright feel like? He was early, the first one to arrive in his class. Mrs. Mattson wasn't even there yet.

He heard shouts coming from across the hall, from Mrs. Pott's room. He left his lunch in the cloakroom at the back of the classroom and walked tentatively out into the hallway. He looked into the room to see most of the class dressed as pirates. Some were having sword fights while others were pretending to walk the plank. He saw a huge treasure chest filled with gold foil-covered chocolate coins. The kids were laughing and having a great time. Three students were at the back of the class, not in costume, rehearsing their lines. He did not see a sad or mad face in the entire classroom. Every student in the class was at school early, and every student in the class was so happy! This class was certainly having a lot more fun with their play than his class was having with their operetta.

He returned to his classroom and sat in his seat, still the only student in his classroom. He looked up at the clock. The bell would ring in less than five minutes, but where was everyone else?

Mrs. Mattson came into the room. "Good morning, Nicholas," she said.

Right then, several students came into the room and took their seats. Mandy came through the door and lingered by Nick's desk for a moment.

"Hi, Nick," she said. "Are you okay? You don't look so well."

"It might be the play," he said.

"I'm a little nervous, too," she said, not correcting him. He was well aware that he should have said 'operetta' instead of 'play,' but she didn't say anything about that. She was just concerned about him. He liked that. "We will be okay, I promise. We get to dance together!" She gave him one of those special smiles that she reserved only for him.

Nick and Mandy were both happy with the dancing in the operetta. The way they danced the glow-worm, before the Prince danced with Cinderella, as the dancers moved in and out, they changed partners. As fate would have it, Nick and Mandy were matched up as partners with each other longer than they danced with anyone else, because of the way the music was played. At the beginning of the song, the dancers were matched up with their original partners, then they changed partners with each phase of the 'glow.' When Mandy was Nick's partner, the music changed and he got to dance with her, with his arm around her for a couple of minutes before the last part of the song when they went back to 'glowing' again. Those minutes while dancing with Mandy were the most magical time of the entire operetta. Each time they practiced the dance, every day for more than a month,

Nick would think of something special to say to Mandy. He told her things like, she was pretty, she danced very well, and one time he even said that he really liked her.

When the time came for Nick to dance with Cinderella, after the general glow-worm dance, he knew his heart wasn't really in it, but, then, what could be expected from fourth grade dancers who were being forced to perform?

The bell rang and more than half the class was absent. Mrs. Mattson walked slowly to the front of the class.

"Class, I am afraid I have some bad news," she said, looking at her students.

The fourteen students who were in their seats looked at their teacher expectantly, wondering what the bad news could possibly be.

"Our Cinderella has the Chicken Pox," Mrs. Mattson said.

"Does that mean the play is off?" Victor asked, a little too enthusiastically.

"It's an operetta, you oaf," said Mark, who sat directly behind Victor, slapping him on the back.

"Does that mean the OPERETTA is off?" Victor asked, mocking Mark.

"No, the show will go on," Mrs. Mattson said, giving a stern look at Victor, "even though we have 19 students out with the Chicken Pox. We'll just have to pick someone else to be Cinderella, and we'll have fewer dancers and a very small choir."

"I'm sorry, Mrs. Mattson," Debbie said. "I didn't mean to make everyone sick." She had come to school three weeks ago with the Chicken Pox, unknowingly, and had then stayed home for two weeks, after exposing the entire class to them. The only student in the class who hadn't been exposed to the Chicken Pox was Mandy, who had been out all that week with strep throat. Some of the students had already had Chicken Pox, so they were immune. They were the ones sitting in the class, along with Nick, who suddenly noticed that he had several red bumps on his arms. They started itching immediately, while he was looking at them.

"It's not your fault, Debbie," Mrs. Mattson said, even though everyone knew it really was her fault.

"Mrs. Mattson?" Nick said, as he raised his hand.

"Yes, Nicholas?" she said, wondering what else could possibly go wrong today.

"I think I better go to the nurse," he said.

"Oh, my goodness!" she exclaimed when she looked at him. "You have pox all over your face."

Nick got up to leave the classroom, glancing at Mandy, who was looking at him with a worried expression on her face. He stopped before leaving the room and told Mrs. Mattson, "I guess you'll have to find another Prince, too."

"Oh, heavens, yes," Mrs. Mattson said, clearly flustered.

The nurse sent Nick home and he was so disappointed that he would have to miss being in the operetta. He was sure Mrs. Mattson would pick Mandy to be Cinderella now – who else could fill the shoes of a princess? And now, he couldn't be her Prince.

MANDY

When I get to work, I see the library has been rearranged again. I'm not sure if this arrangement makes any sense. I overhear two of my co-workers saying the library should be the hub of the school, with all the media and resources easily available to everyone. I agree with that statement, but I don't see how this arrangement is going to help.

My desk has been pushed to one side of the aisle, but now the students will have to walk around me to get to the books in this area. I notice Michelle's desk has been pushed to the other side of the same aisle, up near the front of the library. This is going to make our communication difficult. We need to be closer to each other. Why have they moved our desks out of the library office?

I sigh, resigning to the ridiculousness of the decisions of the Board. They never consult us to find out what is best for our students. I get as much work done as possible, with the students pushing around my desk that's now in their way. I am going to have to move it, not for our convenience, but for the sake of the students. I get quite a lot of paperwork done. I am both surprised and relieved that students are not interrupting me today. Could this new arrangement really be better? Or is it just that the students do not need my help today?

My new supervisor, Frankie, comes into my area of the library. He is very handsome, with his dark hair and dark eyes, and I have had a little crush on him, even though I know he is gay. He has been in theater and on stage for years, and I have seen him perform many times. He has no experience working in schools or with students. I wonder why he would want this position. I figure the steady salary was probably the deciding factor.

"So, they moved your desk, too?" Frankie asks, almost sympathetically. I realize I don't need to complain to him – he understands my situation.

"Yes, and I think it might be too close to this side," I say, standing up, feeling a little excited to have such a neat supervisor to replace the dead-head guy we had for too many years.

"They moved me to a new office, too," he says. "It's over that way, through there." He points in the direction and I realize they have moved him into the old maintenance shop, another senseless decision. "Come on, I'll show you where I am."

I could tell him I already know where it is – has he forgotten that I have worked here for more than 20 years? – but I would rather get away from my desk and follow him. I am finished with just about everything for the day anyway.

He takes a short cut through the library and is able to squeeze through a space between one of the pillars and a bookshelf. I don't want to try to make that squeeze – he is in so much better shape than I am.

"You can fit," he encourages me, then he sees my hesitation. "Oh, let's go around the other way."

I follow him around the long way – he is not familiar with the layout of our campus – but I don't mind following him a few extra steps. He moves quickly, in kind of a dancing way, ahead of me, not caring what anyone thinks of him, and I hear a couple of the high school girls remark that he is really cute. I smile in agreement and round the corner.

I have lost him, but I know the way to his office. I go out

the side door and cut through the parking lot. It occurs to me that I can start parking in this lot now, since my desk has been moved to this side of the campus.

I glance into the woodshop window and see that it is almost 4:00. Oh, no! I forgot to pick up my boys at 3:00 and take them to the dentist! Usually my husband takes them to their appointments, since his schedule is more flexible than mine, but he is out of town! My cell phone rings, but I can't answer it. I know if I take it from my pocket, it will just fall apart before I can press any buttons. I need to get to the car and figure out where the boys would be right now. They must be waiting in the office at their school. I need to hurry and get there. My supervisor will understand, even though I don't have time to go and tell him right now.

My legs are like rubber and instead of getting closer to the other parking lot, I am getting farther away!

I can't be late, but I am already late!

NICHOLAS
Then

"Nicholas, you have a telephone call," his grandmother said sweetly.

Nick was so bored at home. Sure, he had the Chicken Pox, but he didn't feel all that bad, not since his grandmother had fixed the baking soda bath for him. He wasn't itchy now, he didn't have a fever, and his appetite was normal. He didn't know why he couldn't go to school and be in the operetta tonight, but the doctor had insisted that he had to stay home from school for two weeks, until the illness ran its course. He jumped up and ran to the phone, hoping, praying it was Mandy.

"Hi, Nick," an unfamiliar voice said, a girl's voice.

"Who is this?" he asked. He didn't like the sound of his name coming from this strange person.

"It's me, Janice," she answered. "I'm sorry I can't be in the operetta with you tonight. I have the Chicken Pox."

"Well, I have them, too," he said.

"Oh, I'm sorry," she said, sounding as if she were truly sorry.

"So am I," he said, and he hung up the phone.

It rang again immediately.

"I said I was sorry," he said, thinking Janice was calling him back. He didn't want her to call him. Why wasn't she calling her boyfriend, Victor?

"I'm sorry, too," Mandy's sweet voice on the other end of the line said.

"Oh, Mandy," Nick said, feeling that special excitement that came over him whenever she was near. "I didn't know it was you."

"Are you always sorry when you answer the phone?" she asked.

"No, I just thought–" he began. He didn't want to hurt her feelings by telling her that another girl called him before she did. "It doesn't matter, anyway. What are you doing?"

"I just called to see how you are doing," she said. Her voice had such a joy to it. He could tell she really cared about him.

"Well, it's official," he said. "I have the Chicken Pox."

"Oh, no! I guess you won't be there tonight," she said. She sounded very disappointed. "Three more people went home this week with the Chicken Pox. We only had eleven people in class today. We had to borrow some of the pirates from Mrs. Pott's class, so we will have enough kids for all the roles. We are still doing the play – I mean the operetta. Everyone has a role now."

"Are you Cinderella now?" he asked, knowing she had to be, and feeling a little jealous of the new Prince.

"Nope," she said. She sounded disappointed. "Mrs. Mattson picked Heidi to be Cinderella, because she has blond hair."

"That's not fair," Nick said, secretly happy that Mandy was not Cinderella when he was not the Prince. "You should be Cinderella."

"It's okay," Mandy said. "My mom got me a really nice dress, and she even borrowed a crown from one of her friends for me to wear. I'm still the Queen. Besides, I wouldn't want to be Cinderella unless you could be my Prince."

"Well, you will always be my Princess," Nick said, twirling the phone cord around his finger. "Now you won't have to be my mother," he said with a laugh. She laughed, too. "So, who is the new Prince?" he asked.

"We don't know yet," Mandy said. "Mrs. Mattson couldn't make up her mind, so she said she will tell us tonight. All the boys were at all the rehearsals, so they saw what the Prince has to do. Tony and Tom and Brian have to sing and no one else learned their song, so they have to be the messengers. None of them can be the Prince. And, Jay, the King, oh, he's the worst dancer in the world! Every time we practice the dance, he steps on my foot at least once or twice! He can't be the Prince because he can't dance."

She paused, and Nick didn't know what to say. He tried to think of something, anything, to say during the awkward silence that seemed to stretch for hours.

"I wish you were going to be there tonight," Mandy finally said quietly.

"Me, too," he said, feeling warmed by her statement. He always wanted to be where she was.

"I have to go now," Mandy said. "Bye, Nick."

"Bye, Mandy," he said. He heard the line click. He wished he had been able to say something else to her, to keep her on the phone for a while longer, but she was gone.

At seven o'clock, Nick told his grandmother he was going to bed. She kissed him on the forehead. She and his grandfather had both already had the Chicken Pox, so they were immune to it. They couldn't get it again. He was safe at home and wouldn't infect anyone, especially since his grandmother had put a sign on their front door that said, "Chicken Pox inside – do not enter unless you have had them."

Nick had always been an obedient child, never breaking any rules, but tonight he had to break one. He had to sneak out so he could go watch the operetta. His grandfather was already in bed – he got up at four in the morning to go to his job at the mill – and his grandmother was knitting in the living room. Nick wouldn't be able to go out the front door, since she was right near it, nor the kitchen door, since she could see it from where she was sitting. He would have to climb out his bedroom window.

He was kind of glad his screen had ripped last summer, and, since he had been out of town all summer with his dad, his grandfather hadn't bothered to replace the screen. Nick could just open his window and climb through it.

He struggled with the window. He hadn't opened it in months, and it was stuck. He pulled and tugged until finally, it budged. He was able to get his fingers under it and he inched it up, up, up, until he had it high enough so that he was able to slip through it. He was free! This neighborhood had no fences dividing the yards, so he decided to cut through the backyards rather than to risk being seen on the street. The days were getting longer and it was still light, so he was able to discreetly make his way across the block until he reached 44th Avenue. He was directly across from the school, but he didn't have a ticket to the operetta! The tickets were free and had been given to all the students for their family members, but he hadn't thought to bring one with him.

He knew the four outside doors to the multi-purpose room would be closed and locked, and only the main door to the school would be open. He entered the school and walked down the hall. He looked into the office and saw that it was nearly 7:30, show time. Only a few people were in the halls, walking toward the multi-purpose room. He joined in with the group and followed behind them.

"Ticket?" the boy at the door said. Nick recognized him as one of the sixth graders.

"I forgot it," Nick said.

"You have to have a ticket to get in," the boy said, annoyingly, with a nasally voice.

"I forgot it at home," Nick said, hoping the boy didn't notice the marks on his face, and not wanting to breathe on him. He didn't feel like he was still contagious, but the doctor had said to stay away from people for another week.

"Well, it's not that full," the boy said. "Why don't you wait outside, and if all the seats are not filled by 7:30, you can go inside."

"How about if I just stand at the back?" Nick suggested.

"Yes, yes, I guess that will be all right," the boy said. "Come on in, back this way." He pointed to the back of the multi-purpose room, near the kitchen.

The lights were dimmed. Nick moved along the back wall and found a place to stand where he had a good view of the stage. He was in the dark, so one could see him. He was so anxious to see Mandy in her royal dress and crown.

A loud blast of music started and abruptly stopped. A spotlight was turned on the curtain, the curtain opened a few feet, then the spotlight was turned off. The spotlight went on again and the curtain closed. Behind the closed curtain was a loud crash. The spotlight turned off again. Children in the audience began to laugh. Nick smiled. The play – no, the operetta – was a disaster before it even started.

A loud shrieking sound pierced Nick's ears. The principal, Mr. Richey, began to speak before the spotlight was turned on him.

"Good evening," he said. The spotlight shined directly on his face and he squinted while the light was adjusted to show his entire body. He stood in front of the closed curtain holding a microphone. "Welcome, families and friends, to the fourth-grade production of 'Cinderella.' This is an operetta, which means there will be no dialogue, but we will have lots of dancing and singing."

The crowd began to murmur as a huge mass of people came into the multi-purpose room, arriving late. Mr. Richey stood silently on the stage, waiting for them to take their seats and be quiet.

"When 'Cinderella' ends, we will have a fifteen-minute break, after which we will be treated to the fourth-grade presentation of 'Treasure Island.' The crowd roared. Nick's heart sank as he imagined the reaction of his classmates backstage. It was bad enough that they had to do the sissy operetta, but now the crowd was cheering for the other program and nearly ignoring this one. They had to suffer through this operetta before they could get to the show they really came to see. As his eyes adjusted to the darkness in the room, he noticed about twenty pirates sitting in the audience.

Nick was kind of glad he wasn't in the operetta tonight. He hoped they would hurry and get started. He couldn't be here very long. He had to get home before his grandmother noticed he was gone.

"And now," Mr. Richey said, "We present 'Cinderella.' Oh, before we get started, I must announce, due to an outbreak of the Chicken Pox in Mrs. Mattson's class, we won't be having all the dancers who are listed in your program. The programs were printed up three weeks ago. Also, Cinderella will be played by Heidi Shrimpkin, and the Prince will be played by Victor Booha. Thank you."

Nick was astonished! Victor, the worst student in the class, and also the biggest trouble-maker in the class, got to be the Prince? Well, with so many students out with the Chicken Pox, Nick figured Victor must have been the only boy left. They really should have rescheduled the performance.

The curtain, lights and music somehow came together in the right order and the show began with a song, weakly sung by the now shrunken choir of only twelve students, as the spotlight focused on Cinderella, who was sweeping the fireplace. From the back of the multi-purpose room, the props didn't look all that bad. Nick could not even tell that they were made of papier-mâché. The fireplace almost looked real.

The three messengers of the king marched onto the stage and stopped in the middle, at the front of the stage. Their costumes resembled their Boy Scout uniforms.

"The messengers of the King!" they shouted, more than sang. "The messengers of the King! We are the messengers... of... the... King!"

The audience applauded, interrupting their song. Brian, Tony and Tom continued to sing-shout as they stood, frozen on the stage.

"The King will have a ball! You're invited, one and all! The Prince will dance and then he... will... choose... a... Princess!" The three messengers of the King marched off the stage.

The next song was about the wicked stepmother preparing her three daughters for the ball while forcing Cinderella to clean up after them. The entire dance and song went as rehearsed while the girls put on their flowing robes and silly hats for the ball, while Cinderella looked so sad in the corner, sweeping the floor, not allowed to join in the fun. Nick knew Heidi was acting, but he was glad that Mandy wasn't the one who looked sad like that. The stepsisters and stepmother danced off the stage.

Sally, the Fairy Godmother, came onto the stage amidst a puff of glitter thrown from a bucket that was supposed to be offstage, but the bucket flew on stage and just narrowly missed hitting Sally. It rolled over and stopped next to Cinderella. Heidi stepped over it and her ragged dress got tangled on it, so it made a loud thumping sound. Nick realized that the audience must be thinking this was a comedy, since they had so many opportunities to laugh. He was embarrassed for his classmates, and he was glad that he wasn't up there in front of the audience.

Cinderella stepped behind the Fairy Godmother's big, puffy dress so the audience couldn't see her for a moment. Nick knew this was the time when her rags would be peeled off and her beautiful dress revealed. As the barely audible choir sang, Sally waved her glittery magic wand. Apparently, the removal of the rags was taking longer than planned. The song ended and Sally kept waving the magic wand. When at last Heidi stepped from behind the giant, puffy dress, one of the rags was still attached to her light green ball gown. A hand reached in the window and grabbed the remaining rag and tugged it. Heidi lost her balance for a moment, stumbling to the front of the stage.

The crowd was roaring as the curtain closed, trapping Cinderella in front of the curtain. She backed into the curtain, unaware that it had already closed, and then ran off the stage.

The music to 'Glow-worm' started playing on the record player too early. The curtain was still closed, but the music was playing for several minutes before someone must have grabbed the needle, making a horrible scratching sound in the PA system. The music stopped, the curtain opened to reveal the ballroom set, the curtain closed and the music started again. The curtain again opened as the dancers were scrambling to their places.

Nick's eyes were immediately drawn to Mandy. She looked so beautiful! Her dress was long and flowing, light pink with some kinds of sparkly things around her sleeves, her neck and the hem. She was wearing a sparkly necklace, maybe even real diamonds, and a crown studded with diamonds. Her hair curled around her face and the crown stood out in her brown hair. The smile on her face was enormous. She was probably so nervous, but she looked fantastic. Nick thought she looked a lot prettier than Cinderella! Well, she was the Queen, after all.

The dancers began to move in and out as they danced around in a circle. Nick could see what Mandy meant about Jay, the King, being a terrible dancer. He was the only one out of step. As each set of dancers came to the front of the stage, one person had to step backwards down the five steps that led to the front of the stage, then step up again, since the stage wasn't wide enough from front to back. They had only been able to rehearse on the stage for a few days, after the athletic equipment had been moved off the stage. All the other rehearsals had been on the floor of the multi-purpose room. Nick could see how much more difficult this was, as each couple had their turn to come to the front of the stage. Mandy and Jay were the next couple at the front of the stage. Nick saw Jay step on her foot, and she stumbled, but recovered, causing a smattering of laughter from the audience. As the dancers moved about, Nick saw that Mandy would be the one to dance backwards down the steps and not Jay. Jay would be backing up into the center of the circle. Nick was sure that had been planned, since Jay was so uncoordinated.

Jay and Mandy moved with the circle of dancers until they were in the front of the stage and Mandy's back was to the audience. As she began to step backwards, down onto the first step, Jay stepped forward with her, instead of stepping back with the rest of the dancers on the inside of the circle. He stepped on the edge of Mandy's royal gown, which was still on the stage as she was dancing down the steps. Her body jerked a little, held by her dress, and Jay suddenly stepped back as he realized his group was going back into the center of the circle. Mandy, now released, fell, and she tumbled backwards in slow motion, down the steps. The entire audience could see her underwear, as her full dress completely opened to her waist and she ended up sitting on the floor, right in front of the first row of chairs, with the skirt of her dress up over her head. She sat there for a moment while the audience was roaring. The glow-worm music and dance continued as if nothing were wrong. Jay kept on dancing, and Nick could see the huge grin on his face. Jay wasn't even sorry that he had knocked her down the steps! Mandy was struggling to pull her dress down where it belonged, but it looked like it was caught in her crown.

Why wasn't anyone helping her? Nick couldn't leave his hiding place – he wasn't even supposed to be there!

Finally, Mandy's mother was kneeling beside her, fixing her dress, talking to her, helping her stand up and get back up the steps into the circle of dancers. The timing was just right so that as Jay was again at the front of the stage, Mandy danced up the steps and took her place in front of him. As she continued moving in the circle, Nick could see that she wasn't smiling any more. She was probably doing all she could to not cry.

Nick couldn't stand it anymore. He felt crushed for Mandy! He was so mad at Jay! He quickly slipped across the back of the multi-purpose room and out the door to the hallway. He darted across the hall, out the door, and ran all the way home.

It was a lot harder climbing in his bedroom window than it had been to climb out of it. The ground was so low. He couldn't reach the windowsill very well. He needed to find something to stand on, but they had nothing in the back yard!

He stretched his arms as high as he could, so he could just reach the windowsill, and he jumped. His shoes scraped loudly against the house as he slid down, his feet landing in the garden. He had to be quiet! He tried again to jump up so he could climb into his window, but it was no use. He couldn't do it! He felt so weak! Maybe because he hadn't had much of an appetite since he came down with the Chicken Pox, he had no strength.

Nick had no choice. He gave up. He walked around to the front door and softly knocked, trying to think of how he was going to explain himself.

His grandmother opened the door and unlocked the screen door. She didn't seem surprised to see him!

"Did she look pretty in the dress?" she asked, knowing where he had been, as if he hadn't done anything wrong, as if it were normal for him to be coming in the front door after saying he was going to bed an hour ago. He gave his grand-mother a hug and started crying.

JAMIE
Now

The nurse told Jamie he could see Amanda, so he silently slipped into her room after everyone else left. He moved close to the hospital bed, slowly, so he wouldn't disturb her. He knew she was in a coma, but he felt that she was aware of his presence. At any second, her eyes would pop open and she would grab his wrist with a real "Gotcha!"

She didn't move. He noticed that she wasn't wearing any jewelry, but he had read in the paper that she was married – until the accident. Now she was a widow. Where was her wedding ring? Oh, they must have removed it here at the hospital, put away for safekeeping.

He stepped closer to her, so he could see her face clearly. She was still so pretty, with that soft, brown hair, although it was now short, and her curls were all tangled. He could still see the scar on her chin from her bike accident – could that really have been more than 30 years ago? She didn't really look all that much different now than she did then.

Would she recognize him when she opened her eyes? His hair had gone prematurely gray, but he still had the same boyish smile as when she had known him.

"Hey," he said gently. He waited for a response, but she didn't move a muscle. "Remember me?" he asked. "Yeah, it's me, Jamie. I came to see about you, and here you are, in the hospital again. You are really accident-prone, aren't you?" He laughed, paused, waiting for her reaction. He would have to do all the talking now. Before, she had done all the talking, and that had been one of his mistakes. He couldn't think of himself as that shy boy who liked her – he had to be a man and be strong.

"Amanda, I'm here for you again. This time I forgot to bring the ring, but here you are, again, and here am I."

JAMIE
Then

Jamie finally found the cafeteria. He had overheard some ninth graders giving directions to some other new seventh graders, and they had either given the wrong directions or he had misunderstood the details, and he had gotten lost. The atmosphere in the cafeteria had a dull roar hanging in it, every student talking at the same time. Jamie looked at the lunch line and was pleased to see they were offering an alternative to the thirty-five-cent split pea soup and ham meal: for fifteen cents, he could buy a Creamsicle ice cream bar or a Drumstick nutty sundae in a cone.

As he stood in the long line, where, apparently most of the junior high students were buying their noon meal, he looked for Amanda. This was so different from grade school, where they picked up lunch at the kitchen and carried it back to their classrooms to eat. Here was a definite division: all the boys sat on one side of the cafeteria, and all the girls sat on the other side. He saw Amanda at a table of girls, of course, sitting by that noisy girl, Mindy. Mindy had been in three of his classes so far, and he had only one class with Amanda. That was just his luck. He could never sit by Amanda in this divided lunchroom, unless he wanted to be ridiculed for the rest of his life by both the girls and the boys. He would have to find Jerry and sit by him.

He saw Amanda catch his eye, and he, so coolly, looked away from her. He wasn't brave enough to be teased on this first day of junior high. It was bad enough that he was having such a hard time finding his way around the school. He didn't need to add the torture of being teased.

He bought a Drumstick cone and walked over to the boys' side of the cafeteria. He found Jerry at a table that was not too far from where Amanda was sitting. Jamie sat across from Jerry, positioning himself so he could look at Amanda without being noticed.

"Get any good teachers?" Jerry asked, with a mouthful of sandwich.

"I dunno," Jamie replied. He acted as if he were staring off into space, but he was really staring, between Jerry and about four other kids, directly at Amanda. She didn't notice him.

"Hard to tell on the first day, who's good or not," Jerry said. He opened his little bag of potato chips. "I have woodshop for homeroom. Can you beat that?"

"With a stick," Jamie said, an automatic response to this question Jerry always seemed to be asking him.

"Are you gonna try out for any sports?" Jerry asked.

"Are you kidding?" Jamie asked, finally getting the wrapper off his cone.

"I'm going to play JV football," Jerry announced.

"Hmmm," Jamie answered, his mouth full of nuts and chocolate. He zeroed in on what was happening at Amanda's table, where all the girls were laughing at Mindy.

"And so, I told him, I've never even been to France!" Mindy said, her face wide with her smile.

All the girls were laughing hard, leaning to the left and right. Amanda was eating a sandwich that had been cut into little triangles, the way a mom would do, with great care for her child.

"So, I found out about the pecking order in here," Jerry was saying.

"Pecking order?" Jamie asked, completely lost in this conversation.

"Yeah, the more popular you are, the farther back that way you get to sit," Jerry explained. "Pretty soon, I heard, the popular boys and girls will sit at the same table, back there. We are about as far away as we can get."

"Maybe when you join the football team, you'll move up," Jamie said, biting into his cone and still watching Amanda.

"Like I care," Jerry said, shrugging.

"Yeah, me too," Jamie said. He saw Mindy turn to one of the skinny girls, one with a zit-covered face and say something. The other girls at the table again laughed, but Amanda wasn't laughing.

"Stop picking on her, Mindy!" Amanda insisted.

"Did you know your pimple has come to a head?" Mindy asked loudly. The laughter at the table suddenly stopped and the skinny girl's face turned a bright red color as she lowered her head. Mindy lifted her milk carton and began drinking through the straw.

"Melinda Jane!" Amanda said. "When will your *brains* come to *your* head?"

Everyone at that table froze, wondering what their new leader was going to do about this insubordination. Mindy's face turned bright red as her cheeks began to swell and her eyes bugged out. An explosion of milk came from her mouth, and she sprayed nearly everyone at three tables.

"Hey, watch it!" someone yelled.

Mindy narrowed her gaze and looked at each girl at her table, one at a time, then she rested her eyes on Amanda.

"Amanda Lynn," she said seriously, "I told you not to ever call me that."

"It's Amanda Dawn," Amanda corrected, looking just as serious as Mindy.

Mindy burst out laughing and began slapping the table with the palm of her hand. "Amanda Lynn! Get it? She's a mandolin!"

Every girl at the table was silent, holding their collective breath, waiting to see what Amanda was going to do or say.

"No, I was just kidding!" Mindy slapped the table again and again, busting her gut as she was cracking up. The followers at the table all started laughing again, relieved that the tension was broken.

"You better be," Amanda said, looking straight at Mindy.

The girls at the table immediately hushed and sat tensely as they waited to see what was going to happen next.

"It's okay," Mindy said to the girls, "Mandy and I have been friends forever."

"At least since the fourth grade!" Amanda said, and all the girls laughed again.

"Three years IS forever," one girl said, nodding in an exaggerated manner.

Amanda looked right at Jamie, as if she had known all along he was watching her, and she smiled shyly and winked at him. Jamie quickly looked away, checking behind him to see if she may have been winking at someone else, as he finished his cone.

"Gotta go wash my hands," he said to Jerry. "All sticky."

"Well, we only have six minutes until our next class. What do you have after lunch?"

Jamie took his schedule out of his pocket, raggedy from

being pulled out, examined and stuffed in his pocket so many times today. "I have P.E. next."

"Me too, I'll come with," Jerry said.

As they stood up from the table, Jamie definitely saw Amanda giving him a little smile. He smiled, too, wondering if he would ever be brave enough or popular enough to sit at her table.

MANDY

Mindy wants me to go for a ride with her on her mini-bike, but I am afraid.

"Let's just ride our bikes to Chalet Mall," I suggest. On a regular bicycle, I am confident, but I know she doesn't really like to ride up the hill to her house on the way home.

"No!" she insists. "This is the best time for us to ride mini-bikes in the fields."

We hike up the hill across the street to a large field that only has clumps of sagebrush and lots of dirt with trails that she has created with her mini-bike.

"Come on, get on the back!" she instructs. She is kind of bossy, but we are friends, so I usually do what she tells me to do.

I get on and she starts the bike. She gives it too much gas, pops a wheelie, and I fall of the back, landing on my bottom in the dirt. I am not hurt, but she doesn't notice I am not on the mini-bike. She goes nearly a block before turning back to see me still sitting here. She begins laughing so loudly, I can hear her over the noisy bike. She rides back to where I am.

"What are you doing?" she asks, between guffaws.

"I fell off!"

"Why did you do that? Oh, forget it, you don't know how to ride a real bike." She rides down the hill to her driveway and turns off the motor, as I trot dutifully behind her. She puts the bike into its place in her garage and she brings out a golf ball and golf club.

"I'm going to teach you how to putt," she says, dropping the ball in the grass in her front yard.

"I already know how to putt," I say, completely uninterested, but knowing that Mindy always gets her way.

"Okay, stand here, by me, and I'll show you," she says.

I stand to her left, and she practices swinging, back and forth, keeping the club low, just above the blades of grass, before she hits the ball. "You have to practice, so you know how hard you are going to hit and how far it is going to go. Pretend the hole is right over there, and I will make a hole-in-one."

She suddenly lifts the club as if she is teeing off, the club hits the ball, sending it into the next-door neighbor's yard, and she follows through until the club firmly smacks me on the left side of my face. I fall to the ground, seeing stars.

Her dad comes running out of the house and yells at me for standing too close to her while she's swinging. I want to tell him she was only putting, but my face is hurting, pulsing, hot, and anyway, I am afraid of him.

I think I see Jamie across the street, by the bushes, watching us. His eyes are about as big as his face, he looks so scared. I wish he would come over to comfort me. It wasn't my fault! She said she was putting!

EARNEST
Now

Earnest Miller arrived at the church early, before anyone else was there. He let himself in with the key that had once been his mother's – he had never bothered to return it to the pastor after she died. He hadn't thought he would ever need it, but now he was so glad he had it.

Everything was in place for the service: the flowers, the extra podium, the three caskets; one full-size and two small ones.

He couldn't help it – he began to cry. The two small caskets meant two young boys would never grow up, would never graduate from high school and college, would never have families of their own. Earnest was angry with the drunk driver who had taken their lives, the drunk driver who, according to the news report on the Internet, had walked away from the scene of the accident unhurt, unaware of what he had just done. Even if that guy was going to be locked up for the rest of his life, these three people that Earnest loved would never be able to finish their lives.

Something wasn't quite right in here. The flowers were off balance. There were too many arrangements on the left side of the altar, not enough on the right side. He had to fix it before people started to arrive. He wondered who would get here first: the pastor's wife or the minister who would be conducting the service.

After balancing the flower arrangements, he walked again to the back of the sanctuary to take another look. That was much better. The room didn't seem lopsided now. He sat down in the last pew and began to cry again, this time for Sister Peoples, his pastor's wife. He hadn't seen her come to the church since the accident. He had called their house once and left a message, but she hadn't returned his call, which was very unusual. If she had arrived at the church before he had, she would have straightened up the flower arrangements. She would have brought the sanctuary into balance.

Earnest was so thankful he was living across the street from the church, so he didn't have to rely on anyone else for transportation. He needed to be here, right now. He bowed his head and began to pray.

EARNEST
Then

"Pastor Peoples is going to pick you up," his mother said on the phone. "It makes no sense for me to drive all the way out to your house and then all the way back and park in my own driveway and then we both walk across the street to the church. That makes absolutely no sense at all."

"You said you were coming to get me," Earnest said, feeling uncomfortable with this change in plans, which had been made without his knowledge or consent.

"I just told you, Pastor will pick you up," she insisted. "I already talked to him and he said it's no problem for him. He will come by at about 9:15 and get you, so you can be on time for Sunday School."

"Why are we going to Sunday School?" he asked. He hadn't been to church since he was a small boy, and he didn't think he should have to catch up in Sunday School where he left off in the second grade. "I'm not a kid anymore," he reminded his mother.

"The Baptists have Sunday School for all ages," she explained. "I'm going to be teaching the adult class, starting tomorrow. It's about time we had a teacher that knows the Bible, and not have to put all that on Pastor and his wife. So be ready at 9:15, or, no, make it 9:10, so you won't make him late for church."

Earnest knew better than to argue with his mother. She always had the last word and she was always right.

By 9:00 on Sunday morning, Earnest was ready and waiting for his ride. He was hoping they would get to church before his mother arrived, but he knew she was always early and could get in with her own key.

The doorbell rang at exactly 9:10 and Earnest jumped up and ran to the door. He had met Pastor Peoples before at his mother's house, which was right across the street from the church. The pastor was so friendly and joyful, Earnest decided right then that he would one day visit his church, as soon as he got ready. Today, he was ready. He opened the door.

He was not ready for the beautiful young lady who was standing on his doorstep. He resisted the urge to panic.

"Brother Earnest?" she asked. He liked the way she said his name, so safely.

"Yes?" he said. On second glance, maybe she wasn't so young, but she was so beautiful.

"Are you ready for church?" she asked. He must have looked confused because then she continued, "Oh, I'm Sister Peoples, Pastor Peoples' wife. He had to pick up some people in Portland, so I hope it's okay that we came to get you, the boys and I, I mean."

"The boys?" he asked. He was uncomfortable, caught off guard. He felt like retreating back into his apartment. He began to sweat.

"We have two sons, Caleb and Joshua. They are twins," she explained. Her smile was bright and genuine.

"Oh, yes," he said, forcing himself to go with the new plan. "Let me get my Bible."

"I'll wait for you in the car," she said. "I don't like to leave them alone in there for too long."

His heart skipped a tiny bit when she said she would

wait for him, but he dismissed the feeling, grabbed his Bible and his keys and went outside. He closed and locked the door, checking once, twice, three times, to be sure it was locked. He said out loud, 'the door is locked,' so he would remember and not doubt himself later: his door truly was locked. He saw the two boys sitting in the back seat. He got into the passenger's seat of the car.

"Who are you?" one of the boys immediately asked.

"Caleb," Sister Peoples said, "that is not the polite way to introduce yourself."

"My name is Caleb," the boy said. "Who are you?"

"I'm Earnest," he said, smiling. "It's nice to meet you."

"I'm Joshua!" the other boy said. "I know your name. It's Earnest."

"Brother Earnest," Sister Peoples said.

"That is correct," Earnest said, looking straight ahead. He liked the new name she had given him. He could feel Sister Peoples looking at him, glancing at him while she was driving, and his head was getting really hot. He could never look anyone in the eye, especially not a girl, especially not a pretty girl – or lady – like she was. He could feel the energy coming from her body, even though they were not touching – her right arm was at least a few inches from his left arm. He tried to will himself to stop sweating.

He didn't like riding in a car because he had no control over it. He didn't drive because the cars in the other lanes were too distracting, and he couldn't be sure if they were going to stay in their own lanes or not. He preferred to remain in his apartment as much as possible, where he kept things balanced and in order, and unexpected things rarely occurred. He directed his gaze out his side window, where he didn't have to see the traffic and he couldn't see *her* out of the corner of his eye.

"What do you do?" one of the boys asked. Earnest didn't know if it was Caleb or Joshua.

"What do I do?" he asked, unsure of what he meant. He didn't like not knowing which boy was speaking.

"That's what I said," the boy said.

"Boys, don't bother Brother Earnest," their mother told them. "Here we are," she said, as she pulled the car into the church parking lot.

Earnest was so relieved. He had to get out of that car; he was burning up! He pretended not to notice Sister Peoples, but he couldn't help being aware of the patient way she was talking to and waiting for her sons. He could see she really loved them. She was so helpful, just the way a mother should be.

As he entered the church, he saw that only one other person was already there – his mother.

"Good morning," he said, hoping for some tenderness from her, like Sister Peoples was giving to her sons.

"Good morning, Earnest," his mother snapped. He could tell by her tone that she was about to start in on him. "You should arrive earlier. We are going to be starting in less than ten minutes. Is that what you're wearing today? Do you really think tan and brown are appropriate for church? Where is your tie? It's a little warm out for a sweater today, don't you think? Come up here, let me straighten your jacket. Where is your Bible? Oh, there, you have it. I didn't see it at first. Why didn't you bring the one I gave you? Here, come and sit in the front row. That's my stuff there. You can sit right there until I finish teaching the class. Get a copy of the lesson from Sister Peoples so you can read it before we start. You need to ask her if she can buy you a Sunday School book, so you can take it home and read the lesson in advance. I start reading on Monday, and I study the lesson all week, so I can bring all my knowledge to class on Sunday."

Earnest was so embarrassed by his mother's comments. He hoped Sister Peoples hadn't heard her. He did not want to sit in the front row, so he slipped into one of the back pews and sat. Before his mother could reprimand him, Sister Peoples and her sons came into the sanctuary.

"Good morning, Sister Miller," the pastor's wife said with a friendly voice. She went over and gave his mother a hug. The boys quietly scrambled out a side door to another part of the church.

"Good morning, Sister Peoples," his mother said with that false friendliness. He was so glad to hear that tone of voice. It meant she wasn't going to bother him anymore, she had moved on to other things.

"Good morning!" Pastor Peoples said enthusiastically, as he came into the church with several other people. "This is the day that the Lord has made, and I will rejoice and be glad in it!"

Earnest recognized that as a phrase from the Bible. He really needed to read his Bible more, so he could learn it better. He wanted to be able to greet people with a nice phrase like that, on the rare occasions when he did greet people.

The class started, and Earnest was impressed by the content Sister Peoples added to the lesson, the spiritual insight she had. He was ashamed that he didn't know more about the chapter they were studying. He made a commitment right then that he would spend some of his time every day reading and studying the Bible.

After the lesson was the morning worship service. Earnest enjoyed the music and he paid close attention to everything Pastor Peoples was saying. He took notes during the sermon, so he could study it again later, at home. At the end of the service, he knew what he had to do. He belonged here, with this church family. When the pastor gave an invitation for visitors to join the church, Earnest went forth to become a member. Pastor Peoples was now his pastor, and now Earnest had a permanent connection to him – and to his pastor's wife.

"I'm so glad you decided to join our church family," Sister Peoples said in the car, while driving him home.

"I had to," he said, looking out the side window so as not to see her looking in his direction. "I just felt it, from inside me. I guess it was the Holy Spirit, telling me that is my church home."

"That is so wonderful," she said, then she fell silent as they continued to his apartment. The boys in the back seat were strangely silent as well. Earnest could think of a handful of things to say, but he was too bashful, so he just kept staring out the side window.

As they pulled into his driveway, he reached for the door handle.

"Thank you so very much for the ride," he said.

"Welcome to our family," she replied with a smile.

Earnest got out of the car, aware that she stayed in the driveway until he was safely inside his house. He watched through the peephole as she left, where he knew she couldn't see him. He felt so good, so loved, so right, he knew he had done what God wanted him to do. He made up his mind to go to church every Sunday, and he would start preparing right now, by reading his Bible.

MANDY

I am near the Columbia River, looking across to the Oregon side, and I see a short, wide waterfall. Why have I never noticed it before? I have been up and down the highways on both sides of the river, and this is the first time I have seen this beautiful waterfall. I focus my hearing and can hear the crashing of water, like the sound of ocean waves at the beach.

I need to take a picture of the beautiful scene! I pull out my camera, and on the screen, the waterfall is so tiny, I don't think it will show up in the picture. How can I get closer? I can't step off this cliff and into the river to get a better shot. Even when I zoom in, the waterfall is almost gone. I see people swimming near the waterfall. Isn't that dangerous? How are they just swimming in the river like that? I want to swim, but I am so far away. I would settle for a picture of the waterfall. I put the camera in my pocket so I can look at the waterfall, and it is now buried! The river is rising, yet the swimmers are not noticing.

Now I am late, so I need to leave. Maybe I can get the perfect shot of the waterfall if I come back tomorrow. Waterfalls are so beautiful.

JAMIE
Then

Jamie rushed to wait by his bike after his last class. He couldn't leave until Amanda came and unlocked their bikes. He was planning to ride part of the way home with her. He might even follow her and go to her house. Her mom was probably at home waiting for her, maybe with a snack ready.

Jamie wondered where his mother was. She didn't love him enough to stay home and fix an after-school snack for him. When he went to school on his first day of kindergarten, she left the family and never came back. His two older sisters, Misty and Tiffiny, were waiting for him outside his classroom. He was so excited to tell his mother all about his teacher and the new kids in his class. Instead, as they walked home, Misty told him that their mother had gone on a vacation. Jamie couldn't imagine that she would go anywhere without him.

They walked the rest of the way home without talking. When they arrived at the house, Tiffiny, through her tears, made a tuna sandwich for Jamie, just the way he liked it, with mayonnaise and tuna, no relish or pickles, and Misty let him have a whole bottle of Coke for lunch.

Jamie remembered his dad's expression when he came home from work at the hospital that evening: the fallen, defeated look that lasted just a few seconds before he put on his firmness mask, the one he had worn ever since that day. Jamie had waited for his mother's vacation to end, but she never came back home. His dad and his sisters didn't talk about her any more. Jamie wondered what he had done to make his mother go away.

Jamie saw Amanda coming down the steps to the bike racks, giggling at something that noisy girl, Mindy, was saying. Amanda and Mindy were obviously friends. Jamie had four classes with Mindy, only one with Amanda, so he had already been exposed to Mindy's unusual personality on this first day of school. Mindy was so loud, her voice booming, then she would scrunch up her face, as if trying to take it all back, turning it into some kind of laugh explosion. Jamie couldn't see why Amanda was her friend, but maybe it was like his friendship with Jerry. Jerry was outgoing and friendly, while Jamie was quiet and shy, but they made a good pair, so comfortable around each other for the past few years.

Amanda looked over to the bike racks and at first seemed a little surprised to see Jamie standing there, but her look of surprise quickly turned into a shy smile.

"Hi, Jamie," she said, looking directly at him.

"Who's that, your new boyfriend?" Mindy asked loudly, accusingly.

Jamie's heart leaped within his chest.

"No, that's just Jamie," Amanda said.

Jamie was a little disappointed, feeling like 'just Jamie,' and not Amanda's boyfriend.

"Oh, yeah, you sit in front of me in math," Mindy shouted at Jamie.

Jamie nodded, not wanting a conversation with Mindy, just with Amanda.

"I can't believe you rode your bike on the first day," Mindy said to Amanda.

"I didn't want to ride the bus and get here at 7:00," Amanda said.

"You can come to my bus stop," Mindy suggested. "Our bus doesn't come until 7:45 and we get to school at 8:00."

"Yeah, then I'd have to walk a mile to your bus stop," Amanda said, "and then get here at 8:00, twenty-five minutes before class starts."

"Better than getting here at 7:00!" Mindy shouted. "I'm going to go sign up for pep club. Wanna come?"

"Not today," Amanda declined. "I'm going to ride home now. I can sign up in the morning."

"Okay, it's your loss!" Mindy yelled, as she turned and scampered back up the steps. "Good luck riding uphill, ALL the way home!"

JAMIE
Now

"You know, it's funny. I still don't know how to start a conversation with you. You always started it, and I just went along with you. All the way here – I drove from Yakima to get here to you – I was thinking of all the things I never told you, all the things I've always wanted to tell you. When we were kids, I wanted to tell you so many things, but I just never had the chance. Most of the time you were talking, but when you weren't talking, I was just waiting for the next thing you would tell me.

"Over the years, all those years while we were apart, every time anything happened, I wanted to tell you even the small stuff – especially the small stuff, because you were always so interested in the details.

"So, now I'm here, here we both are, and you can't say anything right now; so, now I'm starting. I'm trying to start, anyway.

"You must know you have always been so special to me. You were the only girl who talked to me in junior high. I'da thought I was invisible to girls, if you didn't talk to me.

"Ever since our first day in seventh grade, you made me feel welcome to Wilson. You just came into my life and became my friend. I didn't even have to do anything to try to make you like me. You liked me, right off the bat. Because of you, junior high wasn't awful for me. As a matter of fact, because of you, junior high was a great adventure."

Jamie settled back in the chair, looking for any type of reaction from Amanda, as he gathered up his courage to talk to her and to tell her what was really on his mind.

"You know the castle house on Yakima Avenue? The one you liked so much? You kept telling me how you wished you lived there, and how the family who lived there must have a fairy tale life. Well, I can tell you, it was no fairy tale living there. I lived there with my dad and my sisters, and you couldn't really call us a family. That was, well, it still is, my house, but I hated it so much, I couldn't bring myself to tell you the truth about living there.

"So, if I didn't have the courage to tell you that truth, how was I ever going to tell you the truth about my feelings for you? Now is our time. Where do I start?"

Just as Jamie was gathering his thoughts, ready to tell Amanda everything, he heard someone coming to the door. What horrible timing! He jumped up and slipped out of the room before this person could see him, or worse, begin to question him.

MANDY

I have been friends with Mindy since the fourth grade, and we always have gotten along, even with our disagreements. She has crazy ideas, and I usually go along with her, like the time she wants us to sing like Karen Carpenter and we record our voices on her new cassette tape recorder. When we listen to ourselves singing, we both think our own voices are really distorted, but the other one sounds normal. Mindy gets so mad at me for saying her voice really sounds like that; yet, on the other hand, we spend forty-five minutes listening and laughing and rewinding and laughing again, so hard we both get side aches. She says she is hyperventilating and when I ask her what that means, she doesn't know, and she just laughs harder, saying she must be doing it or else she would be able to stop laughing.

We spend almost every weekend together: riding the bus and going downtown to the mall; trying to teach ourselves how to play tennis at Mrs. Plath's tennis court, because it is free, and Mrs. Plath never comes outside to chase us away; playing ping-pong in Mindy's basement; walking to the Chalet Mall to get candy and gum; and trying to figure out who we are and what we are going to be when we grow up.

We also spend lots of time together during the summer and after school, in Girl Scouts, softball, pep club, taking advanced swimming lessons and guitar lessons, then trying to play our guitars together, which is kind of a disaster, because neither one of us has rhythm nor an ear for music. We play off-beat in different keys, probably not even playing the same song at the same time, yet we are still determined that we are going to be in a famous band someday. We try our hands at writing songs that are thinly disguised copies of songs by the Beatles or the Carpenters or the Bee Gees and even Peter, Paul and Mary.

And we have sleepovers nearly every Friday night, alternating between her house and my house. My mom provides better snacks, but her house has a full basement where we can live our fantasy lives and not be in the way of the rest of her family. Her parents are a lot older than mine, so they don't like to bother with trudging all the way down all those steps to check on us.

Then in seventh grade, she starts acting differently. I notice that she becomes more interested in the cheerleaders than the football players, even to the point of following her favorite cheerleader, Joyce, around the school. Mindy has become obsessed with her, hanging out around her locker, finding out where she lives, and trying to sit as close as possible to her in the cafeteria so she can eavesdrop on her conversations. I want none of that – I am interested in boys, especially Nick, who keeps coming back to town from Montana just to ignore me. I am so fixated on him, even though he was mean to me, that if he just says one word to encourage me, I would leap into his arms without hesitation. My heart flutters every time I see him, and he still ignores me.

One Friday night the sleepover is at Mindy's house. While we are playing ping-pong, eating frozen pizza, and making a feeble attempt to clean up her room at her mom's insistence, all Mindy can talk about is Joyce. I keep starting conversations about our other interests: our future music career, Mrs. Bennett, our Civics teacher, who picks on us because we challenge her political preferences (she loves Nixon and we don't trust him), our parents, and our classmates, but Mindy brings every conversation back to Joyce.

When her mom tells us it is time for bed, Mindy wants to show me something she learned about boys: that they want to lie on top of girls and kiss them. I can't understand this, but I know right then, this is our final sleepover. She is scaring me. I start avoiding her at school as she becomes more and more popular, with so many new friends.

Later, when I am in an accident with my bike and a car, she doesn't come to see me in the hospital, nor does she sign her name on my cast.

I have been looking for Mindy for a long time, so we can talk, but now I can't find her. I can't find Nick, either. Where are my dear friends going?

EARNEST
Now

The church was packed with mourners dressed in black, with standing room only, and at least fifty people in the foyer. Earnest stayed in the pew near the back, not wanting to make conversation with anyone else. He couldn't see Sister Peoples from where he was sitting, but he knew she had to be there, in the front row. She had lost all three of her family members. It was a miracle that she had survived the accident. He didn't know how she would even be able to cope with or come to grips with what had happened. After the countless times her soothing voice had comforted him, especially when he was on the verge of a panic attack, he wanted to be one who was able to comfort her. He had three scriptures chosen and memorized for when he would be able to talk to her.

Pastor Brown, the associate pastor of their church, took his place at the podium. Earnest was still trying to see Sister Peoples, avoiding looking at the three caskets, which had to be breaking her heart right now. Her husband and her twin sons had died instantly in the accident, so she hadn't had an opportunity to tell them goodbye. She must really be hurting right now.

"Good afternoon," Pastor Brown said, and the low murmuring quieted. "We thank you all for coming today. Before we begin, I would like to ask for your continued prayers for Sister Amanda Peoples, who is still in a coma. For anyone who would like to send flowers or a card, the address of the hospital in Seattle, where she is being treated, is listed in your program."

Earnest went numb. Sister Peoples was in a coma? Why hadn't he heard about this? It wasn't in the article he had read on the Internet about the accident, and he hadn't spoken to anyone about it, so he didn't know! His mind stopped at that point and refused to go forward with what was happening. The remainder of the funeral service was a blur, with the words 'Sister Amanda Peoples, who is still in a coma' repeating in his mind, over and over.

He had to go see her! But she was in Seattle, more than a hundred miles away. How could he get there? He didn't dare tell anyone that he needed a ride. Besides, she was the only person who would have gone out of her way to give him a ride that far away, oh, except maybe her husband. Make that her late husband. There was no way he could get a ride to the hospital in Seattle. How could he possibly get to her?

He closed his eyes and said a prayer for Sister Peoples, then he said a prayer for himself as tears rolled down his face.

EARNEST
Then

Earnest's heart skipped a beat when Sister Peoples entered the sanctuary. He couldn't look directly at her – someone might see him looking – so he focused his eyes on a point across the room. Her dark hair flowed about her as her smile sparkled and her eyes twinkled. As she drifted by him, he caught the scent of her perfume – Tabu. His aunt had always worn Tabu, but this fragrance was so light and intoxicating, not heavy like his aunt's. Still, he recognized Tabu; and how appropriate that Sister Peoples – a married woman – would be wearing it. She was off-limits to him, taboo.

How old was she, anyway? She looked so young, but she had to be at least 40. That would make her a few years younger than Earnest, an acceptable age. What was he thinking? She wasn't available, she was happily married, she was enchanting. Was she trying to put him under her spell? Was she even aware of the effect she was having on him? Why couldn't he have met her years ago, before she met the pastor? He knew he shouldn't be questioning God, and he knew God had a plan for him and his life, so why did she seem to be the one for him, yet, the forbidden fruit? No, he didn't want her only because he couldn't have her. Many of the women at their church were not married, and he wasn't at all attracted to any of them. He just couldn't help falling for Sister Peoples the first time he met her.

This was an interracial church, and the members and

people who attended were of different races. He wasn't coming to church to find romance, although his mother often reminded him that Proverbs 18:22 says, "He who finds a wife finds what is good and receives favor from the Lord." He was coming to church to get peace with God and direction for his life. He had felt an immediate relief when he stepped into the sanctuary, a completely different atmosphere from the outside world: calm, peaceful, welcoming. He had felt the presence of God, something that had been missing from his life for a long time.

As he took his place on the pew beside his mother, tears began to stream down his face. He was glad he was at the far end of the pew, up near the front, so people couldn't see him crying; but he had to cry. He knew he had stayed away from God for too long, and seeking Him at home through his computer had not been the answer. Earnest needed to be in the house of the Lord. He knew his mother would want to introduce him to her church family, but she would follow proper protocol and wait until the appropriate time. The congregation began to sing a joyous song as the pastor came to the pulpit. Tears continued to flow down Earnest's face. He didn't look at anybody but the pastor; he especially could not look at Sister Peoples.

He kept his eyes closed most of the time: during the songs, during the opening prayer, during the welcome the pastor gave. When the invitation to Christ was given at the end of the service, Earnest felt a hand on his left shoulder, pushing him toward the front of the room, (it couldn't have been his mother's hand, she was on the right side of him – no one was physically standing to his left) and he fell on his knees and poured his heart out to God. He asked for forgiveness, he dedicated his life to God's service, he thanked God for loving him and for giving him this opportunity to come to Him. His burden was lifted, and he felt himself being lifted to his feet. The choir began to sing "I'm so glad Jesus lifted me," and Earnest joined the song as he returned to his seat. He didn't sit, though; he and the rest of the congregation were on their feet, singing and shouting and praising God.

When church was over and it was time to go home, Earnest was in love with Jesus, and, he couldn't help it – he was in love with Sister Peoples, too.

JAMIE
Then

Jamie had begun hanging around Westpark shopping center on the chance that he might see Amanda there. She had told him it was the closest shopping center to her house, and she often rode her bike or walked there.

Jamie rode his bike on the sidewalk, all around the shopping center, from Laurent's grocery store, down past the flower shop, by Luv's Hallmark, Parry Jewelers, the shoe store, the tiny tavern and the laundry, all the way to Harmon's Kentucky Fried Chicken. He stopped and stood with his bike for a few minutes, surveying the scene and enjoying the smell of the chicken radiating out of the restaurant. He saw some bikes parked up near Tuft's Drug store, so he got on his bike again and went up the other side of the shopping center, by the yarn shop and the hardware store. Just as he was approaching Tuft's, the door opened, and there she was!

Amanda walked out of the drug store with a tiny sack, which she put in her pocket as she walked over to the bike rack. She must have sensed that he was behind her, because she abruptly turned and saw Jamie, slowly riding his bike, pedaling backwards so he wouldn't go too fast for the sidewalk.

Everything happened so quickly. He saw her face light up, just like she turned on a light inside her head, and her eyes sparkled. He smiled, feeling the sheer delight of finding her, 'by chance.' Then she stumbled over another bike and began to fall backwards and sideways, her hands flying up in the air, her face changing into an expression of surprise mixed with embarrassment. At the same time, Jamie's front tire hit a slick spot on the sidewalk and his bike slid out from under him. They both went to the ground at the same time, just a couple of feet from each other. Jamie's bike pulled him down and then landed on him so he and his bike became entangled with the other bikes in the rack.

She recovered first from her fall. "Are you okay?" she asked, her eyes wide, as she surveyed the scene.

He didn't feel any pain except humiliation. "Yeah... are you?" He tried to disentangle himself and his bike from the other bikes that had crashed with him.

She started laughing and laughing. Her face was so red, and tears started coming from her eyes. She was becoming hysterical! He had to help her.

Jamie tried again to get out of the mess of bicycles, and they were like a Slinky, all interlaced and moving together, against him! Just as he was nearly up, things twisted and turned, and he was down on the ground again, the bikes crashing and forcing him to stay where he was. Amanda was still laughing, laughing so hard. She leaned back, almost lying on the ground, giggling and snickering and chuckling, all rolled into one. He was afraid she was going into shock or something. He had heard his dad talking about people acting strangely when they had an accident, reacting the opposite way they should. Yet her laughter was contagious.

He could not help himself – he started laughing, too. She wasn't stopping, and he couldn't stop either. He was not able to move while he was laughing. He heard the jingle of the door opening behind him and suddenly Amanda stopped laughing. He looked right at her, worried, and stopped laughing, too. A man and lady walked by, not bothering to look down at these two teenagers on the ground. The couple went to their car, a few yards away from Amanda. As soon as their car doors slammed, Jamie and Amanda burst into laughter again.

She was able to get to her feet, still laughing, and she came over to him and began to pull the row of bicycles off Jamie. Together they worked and laughed, and he wiggled out of the mess and stood up. They finally got all the bikes back upright and properly into the rack.

Once the ordeal was over, Jamie wanted to brush Amanda's hair back into place, as it was looking a little wild now, but he kind of liked it that way. Their laughing subsided and they both got on their bikes.

"What was so funny?" Jamie asked.

Amanda's face scrunched up and she giggled a funny-sounding giggle. This started another round of laughter. Some other adults walked by them, and he and Amanda were able to hold it in for a moment, only to explode again once the adults were gone.

"It was funny," Amanda said, slowing down her laughter, "because it wasn't funny! I was falling, and then, in slow motion, you were falling, too, and all those bikes just joined in!" Her face was so red as she got into one of those deep-laugh phases that only good friends can share. Jamie kept laughing right along with her. During the actual fall, he had been afraid she was hurt, but now that he knew she was fine and uninjured, the scene was extremely funny.

"Let's go!" Amanda said suddenly. She jumped on her bike and pedaled toward Kentucky Fried Chicken, which was behind Jamie, so he had to turn his bike around and catch up with her. She rode quickly out of the shopping center by a back road, into a neighborhood, taking the same short cut she took when she rode her bike home from school, but this time instead of going straight on 42nd Avenue, she turned left onto Avalanche Avenue.

This was a wide, quiet street with no traffic. They were flying down the street and out of the corner of his eye, Jamie saw Tony Lagoni standing in front of a yellow Volkswagen. Oh, boy, Tony had a big mouth. Jamie hoped Tony wouldn't tell everyone that he saw Jamie with Amanda. He knew he saw them – he was looking right at them. Maybe they were going so fast that Tony didn't recognize them?

He didn't have time to worry about it now. Amanda was zooming ahead, flying through the intersections of this lazy neighborhood. She rounded the corner and Jamie was right behind her as she jumped the curb onto Gilbert Park. They rode down the grassy hill and she led him to a picnic table in the shade of a huge tree. As they propped their bikes against the table, Jamie noticed that Amanda wasn't even breathing hard.

"What are you doing today?" Amanda asked, taking a seat at the picnic table.

Jamie blushed. "Looking for you," he said truthfully, sitting across from her.

She laughed. "You are so funny," she said, not believing him.

"You made me forget what I was going to do," he said. That was the honest truth. If he had any other plans, they had been abandoned, forgotten, when he thought about Amanda and what she might be doing today. He felt so fortunate to have found her.

"Well, what is there to do today, anyway?" she asked. "I just rode my bike to the store because I didn't have anything else to do."

"Yeah, me, too," he said.

"My parents went to some bowling tournament," she said. "I didn't want to go. I love to bowl, but the bowling alleys are always so smoky inside, you know?"

"Yeah," he agreed, nodding, but he didn't know. He hadn't been inside a bowling alley, not ever.

"They didn't make me go with them," she said. "Do your parents smoke?"

"No," he answered. He knew his dad didn't smoke, but since he didn't know anything about his mother, he didn't know if she had taken up smoking. He knew that she didn't smoke when she lived with them, a hundred years ago.

"You're so lucky," she said, pulling the tiny paper bag from her pocket.

He didn't feel like he was so lucky, regarding his family. She didn't know that he didn't really have a family life at all. But right now, he did feel lucky, lucky to be here with her.

She began to turn the little bag over in her hands, playing with it without thinking about what she was doing. He could see her mind was on what she was saying, not what she was doing. "My dad quit a couple years ago, and I was so glad, but my mom still smokes, and it really bugs me. I keep telling her she should quit, but she won't. I especially hate it when she smokes in the car. I can't get away from it. And when the smoke all comes right to me, like it always does, and I complain about it, Mom says, 'smoke follows beauty,' as if that is going to make it any better."

"Yeah, that must be awful," he sympathized. He didn't want anything to bother Amanda.

"I would invite you over, but I'm not allowed to have boys in the house when my parents are not there," she said.

"That's okay, this is really great, right here," he replied. He looked at the picnic table so he wouldn't have to meet her gaze.

"Want a piece of gum?" she asked, taking a pack of gum out of the little sack and opening it.

"Yeah, sure," he said. He wasn't really much of a gum-chewer, but he would take just about anything Amanda offered him.

"It's Black Jack," she said. "Do you like licorice?"

"Yeah," he lied. He did not like licorice, but he wanted to like what she liked. He really liked her.

"It tastes like licorice," she said. "I love it." She held out the pack to him.

He took a piece and slowly unwrapped it. He had never seen black gum before. Most of his friends liked Chiclets or Juicy Fruit. He put it the little black strip in his mouth and chewed it, following her lead. It tasted awful, but he smiled, a closed-mouth smile while chewing. Amanda really seemed to like this odd gum!

"So, I've seen you coming down Chestnut on the way to school," she said, surprising him. He didn't think she had noticed; but then again, she was very observant. "Do you live up that way?"

"Yeah," he said. He really was not much of a conversationalist, not even with his best friend, Jerry. Most of the time he was with Jerry, Jerry did most of the talking. Amanda didn't seem to notice. That's what he liked about her. She just liked being with him, and he didn't have to talk. She did enough talking for the both of them, and he was fine with that.

"Have you seen that house on Yakima Avenue that's like a castle?" she asked, suddenly very excited. "It is so neat! Whoever lives there must be the luckiest family in town! Whenever we drive by it, I always think about what it's like to live in a castle, like a real princess, or a real royal family. I wish we could go inside it, but I guess a regular family – or a royal family! – lives there. I wish we lived there, you know?"

"Yeah," he said, nodding slowly. He didn't elaborate and let her know that he did know all about it: about the high stone walls, the elegant, landscaped yard, the four balconies, the two tower rooms, and the coldness of the entire castle that even the wall-to-wall carpeting and central gas heating couldn't warm, ever since his mother had left. A castle could never be a home without a mother there to bring it life.

"That has to be the neatest house in the city," she said. "Oh, I guess, except for the Smith Mansion. Do you know Laurie Smith? She's was one of the cheerleaders last year. I guess she lives in a huge mansion, up on the hill, on Scenic Drive. Not near our house, no, we are down in a little poverty pocket below Scenic. Their mansion is way out, way farther west. We drove by it before, but I can't remember exactly where it is."

"There are lots of big houses in town," Jamie said. "What about Congden's Castle?" He wanted to direct her attention away from the coldest castle, the one on Yakima Avenue.

"Oh, yeah, I forgot about that one. I haven't really seen it," she said. "I really love castles. Have you ever been to that one?"

"No," he said, shaking his head, glad for this turn of the conversation.

"Castles are so neat," she said, with a dreamy look on her face. "I would LOVE to live in a castle. Or even to visit one. That would be so cool."

Jamie wondered if it were too soon to dispose of his gum, which hadn't yet lost its flavor. He realized that he had something she wanted so badly to see, but he could not take her to his house, not now, not ever.

"Yeah," he said, his safest answer to just about every question she was asking.

"Have you ever thought about, in just one year we will be driving?" she asked. "Well, we will be in driver's ed, anyway, and starting to drive."

"Yeah," he nodded, even though he hadn't really thought much about it. He didn't like to think that far ahead. He liked to live in the moment, and that was enough for him to contemplate without trying to leap a year ahead in his thinking.

"I feel kind of bad about it," she said, putting her elbow on the table and resting her head on her hand.

"Why?" he asked. His other friends were so eager to start driving, and some already were driving at age 14, but he had never heard anyone say they felt bad about driving.

"Well, look at those cars going by," she said, pointing to the light traffic on Lincoln Avenue. "Look at all those people, going by so fast, hurrying to get from one place to the next, and not caring about their surroundings."

"Yeah," he said, although he didn't really get what she meant.

"I mean, they are going so fast," she repeated. "They are not enjoying the sights and the scents along the way. Like, right here, we can smell the pine trees and the grass. Those guys are so out of touch with nature. When we are on our bikes, we have time to see all the cats and dogs, and we can smell the flowers when we ride by them. I don't want to be one of those people who just zooms through life without enjoying it."

"You won't," Jamie said. He knew that was the truth. Amanda made an effort to enjoy life; she didn't expect great things to just fall into her lap. As a matter of fact, she sometimes acted as if she thought she didn't deserve the life she was living. Well, did anyone deserve exactly what he got? Some kids lived down by the tracks in little trailers that were crowded with love. Some kids lived halfway up the hill, above others, but below the ones who lived on Scenic Drive, who thought they were better than anyone else because they were so rich. Some kids were born into lives of love and abundance, living in a castle, and then the life and love were taken out of the castle when their moms decided to move on to a better life. Which were the ones who deserved they lives they were living? What had those kids done to deserve any of it?

"When we are riding our bikes, we can see butterflies in the summer, and we can smell the lilacs in the spring," Amanda said. "Have you ever smelled the lilacs when you were riding in a car?" she demanded.

"No," he admitted with a smile. He didn't tell her that he never noticed the smell of lilacs, or that he didn't even know what they smelled like.

"See what I mean?" she asked. "We are going to be just like all the other grown-ups, out of touch with nature. I don't want to be like that."

"You don't have to," he said. "You can still ride your bike."

"How many people that have their driver's license do you see riding their bikes?" she asked. "Do you ever see any teachers riding their bikes to school? Do you know any grown-ups who ride their bikes to work?"

"No," he said. Maybe she had a point about that. She was usually right about things like that, things that Jamie never contemplated. He couldn't think of any adult who rode a bike. His dad worked at the hospital only a few blocks from home, well, about ten, but he always drove. Jamie always rode his bike everywhere he went, and why? He rode his bike because he couldn't drive.

"They just don't do it. It seems like everyone has only one mode of transportation," Amanda said. "Once they start driving, they don't go back to a kid way of getting around. Driving is the adult way."

He nodded in agreement.

"I'm burning up," she announced, jumping off the bench. "Let's go put our feet in the irrigation ditch," she suggested mischievously, pointing to the ditch that ran near the edge of the park.

"Doesn't it have a fence around it?" he asked. People were not allowed to be near irrigation ditches. Supposedly they were unsafe, the water was too swift and the cement sides too slick and steep; but some weren't very deep.

"Only on one side," she said, leaving her bike and running over to the ditch. Jamie followed her, walking, though, not running. She kicked off her sandals and sat on the edge of the ditch with her feet hanging into the water.

When Jamie got there, he saw that the water was quite low, only about two feet deep. It was one of the smaller irrigation ditches, one of the in-town kind, about four feet across and three feet deep. He sat on the edge, not too close to Amanda, but near her, and took off his shoes and socks.

"Wow, that's really cold!" he said, as he put his feet in the water.

"Yeah, but it feels good!" she said. "You get used to it fast. Do you think it's a hundred out? I don't. I think it is 94 degrees."

"No, I don't think it's a hundred," he agreed. While they had been in the shade, he felt fine, but now that they were in the sun, he was feeling quite hot. The water did feel good on his feet now, and it was cooling down his entire body. He looked at Amanda's feet. They looked like baby feet, so smooth and little, with her toenails painted a bright pink color.

His mind flashed back to his mother's feet, with her toenails always delicately painted with bright red polish. His mother had always gone barefoot inside the house all year, even on those cold stone floors.

Amanda noticed that Jamie was looking at her feet.

"You know what's weird?" she said, pulling one foot out of the water and holding her leg straight out, letting the water drip from it as she looked at it.

"What?" he said, shaking his head. He didn't want to tell her it was weird that he had run into her on this hot summer day and they were sitting at the edge of an irrigation ditch with their feet in the water, or that she and his mother both polished their toenails, but he did think that was weird.

"It's weird that when I polish my toenails, I always get some nail polish on my toes," she said, splashing her feet in the shallow water. "Okay, that's not the weird part. The weird part is, when I wash my feet, the polish comes off my toes, but it doesn't come off my toenails. I mean, I know nail polish is waterproof, but then, why does it come off my skin and not my nails?"

"I think it's because everything can wash off skin," Jamie said. "Like when I get paint on my hands, at first it won't wash off, then later it does. Or maybe it's because we are always growing new skin and sloughing off the old skin."

"Ew! That's like what a snake does!" Amanda said, shivering. "You sound like Mr. Gural! Do you have him for science, or do you have Mr. Bongers?"

"I have Bongers," Jamie said, trying to stay serious. "But, no, really, that is what our skin does. The old skin comes off, a little bit at a time, and is constantly being replaced by new skin."

"You really do sound like a science teacher," Amanda said accusingly. She kicked her feet in the water, splashing drops across the ditch to the other side.

"I like science," Jamie confessed. "Don't you?"

"It's NOT my favorite class," Amanda said. "Science, bummy science. But I do like Mr. Gural," she said, smiling.

Jamie had heard that from lots of girls at school. Mr. Gural was young and good-looking, and all the girls wanted to be in his class. Mr. Bongers was older, but he was full of information and he always presented it in such an entertaining way. Science was Jamie's favorite class – except for Art, since Amanda was in that class with him. He actually hated Art class; it made no sense and was a waste of time, but Amanda loved it, so that made it more than bearable for Jamie. He loved to look over at her table and see the smile on her face while she was creating something or working on a project.

"Do you think you are going to get a job when you turn 16?" Amanda asked, out of the blue. She was always doing things like that, changing the subject, following her own train of thought. Jamie liked that about her. She never got stuck on one subject.

"I doubt it," Jamie said. He didn't want to tell her that his old man was loaded and he didn't need to work.

"Yeah, it's probably better if we concentrate on school while we are still in school," Amanda said.

"Are you going to get a job when you are 16?" Jamie asked.

"I already have one," Amanda said.

"You have a job?" he asked, surprised. She was so good

in school and she already was working at a job?

"Yeah, baby-sitting the two kids that live next door to us," she explained. "Every Friday and Saturday night, their parents go out, and somehow, about a year ago, I became their permanent baby-sitter. It's really fun, though, because I like to make up stories to tell them, and the girl is seven and the boy is nine, so they don't need a lot of work. After I put them to bed, I can do my homework, and then I usually watch a few TV shows, like 'The Partridge Family' and 'Brady Bunch' on Fridays – those are my two favorite shows – and I like to watch 'Mary Tyler Moore' and 'Bob Newhart' on Saturdays. Then I usually fall asleep until their parents come home at one or two in the morning, and I sleep-walk back to my house. My Mom and Dad always wait up for me. I put all the money in the bank so someday I can buy something really great, or have some spending money when I go to college, if we are not all wiped out by a nuclear bomb before that. Or maybe I'll invest some of my savings in the stock market."

"The stock market?" Jamie asked. "What's that?"

"Oh, don't you have Mr. Smythe for Economics?" she asked. "We are learning all about the stock market. I might even become a stock broker."

"Stock broker? What do they do?" Jamie asked. He hadn't taken Economics yet, so he hadn't been introduced to the stock market. All he knew was about the stock market was that it made his Uncle Barney upset whenever anyone mentioned it, but Jamie didn't even know what it was.

"A stock broker buys and sells stocks for people," Amanda explained, "and every time people buy or sell, they pay the stock broker."

"That sounds like an easy way to make money," Jamie said, wondering exactly what a stock was.

"Yeah, and I read that you can make a lot of money that way," Amanda said. "I plan to become a millionaire someday, before I turn 30, all on my own, NOT by marrying a rich man."

Jamie smiled. He didn't know if his dad had a million dollars, but Jamie did know that one day he would probably become a rich man. Of course, he would want Amanda to love him for who he was, not for being rich, but being rich couldn't hurt. It might even help.

A dog started barking, startling Jamie. He and Amanda looked up to see a huge dog on the other side of the irrigation ditch, behind the chain link fence, barking at them.

"That's a Marmaduke dog," Amanda said.

"What's a Marmaduke dog?" Jamie asked.

"You know, Marmaduke? From the comics? I think he's supposed to be a Great Dane," she explained.

"Hey! You kids!" a man yelled. "What are you doing? Are you aware that you are trespassing?" A big, burly man stepped out of his house, out of Marmaduke's house, into the yard and began to come towards the fence.

Amanda scrambled to her feet, leaning on Jamie to help her stand. She ran back to the park, laughing. She didn't realize until she was a good distance away from the irrigation ditch that she had forgotten to grab her sandals. When she looked back to where they had been sitting, she noticed she had knocked Jamie off-balance, into the irrigation ditch.

He had slipped and fallen all the way down into the water, so he was sitting on the bottom of the cement ditch. The current, although slow, was rather strong, and Jamie had a bit of difficulty getting to his feet, especially since he was laughing so hard. Amanda appeared, giggling hysterically, and held out her hand for Jamie to reach. He grabbed her hand and as she pulled, she lost her balance and fell into the ditch as well. She was standing in the knee-deep water, still holding his hand. He hoisted himself up and they both climbed out of the ditch. Jamie grabbed his shoes and socks, Amanda picked up her sandals, and they began running back to the picnic table where they had left their bikes.

They both fell to the grass, snickering, face-to-face. Amanda fell onto Jamie's arm, as he reached out in an attempt to break her fall. His arm was around her. Her long, wavy hair felt good as it fell across his arm. Her face was so close to his, he suddenly had a feeling he should kiss her. He wanted to kiss her! He looked into her eyes, and she had a mischievous look, along with her killer smile that made him forget important things. She closed her eyes. He thought she was about to kiss him, and his heart raced. He didn't know if he should kiss her or not! He was going to try it. He began slowly moving his face closer to hers.

"Two little love birds, fell out of a tree!" a little kid's voice shouted, "K-I-S-S-I-N-G!"

Amanda quickly pulled herself to a sitting position, still laughing. Jamie sat as well, beside her. A family was bringing their lunch to a nearby picnic table, and the little boy was still watching Jamie and Amanda accusingly.

They sat on the grass and watched the family as they brought their Kentucky Fried Chicken buckets and sacks into the park and began to unpack the containers. Jamie thought that the family looked very jolly. The dad was large and round, like Santa Claus, and the mom was shorter and rounder. Three kids, two girls about ten years old and the younger boy who had teased Amanda and Jamie were all chubby as well. They seemed to be so happy, all together and laughing as they were getting ready to eat.

"My mom says," Amanda said, leaning close to Jamie and speaking in a lowered voice, "that when the whole family is fat, they have poor eating habits. I'm not exactly sure what she means by that, but I think she means that the mom doesn't plan and cook good meals for the whole family, and so they just eat whatever they want, like a lot of junk food, whenever they want."

Jamie kept looking at the family and he still thought they looked very jolly. To be honest, his family had terrible eating habits, but none of them were fat. This may have been because they didn't eat often enough, not just because they didn't eat well-planned and well-cooked meals together. He envied Amanda, knowing from her statement that her mother did plan and cook good meals for the whole family. Nobody did that in his family, not since his mom left home.

Jamie looked back at the man who had yelled at them and saw that he was on the other side of the chain-link fence, laughing his head off at them.

"He just did that to scare us!" Amanda said, looking at Jamie's soaked clothes.

"And it worked!" Jamie added, grinning. The weather was so hot, he was already starting to get dry – and itchy. He scratched his legs with his nubby fingernails, then he reached up and scratched both arms at the same time.

"We have to get you to some house water," Amanda said. "Otherwise, you will be itching all afternoon."

"No, I'm okay," Jamie said. Every part of him except for his head had been in that dirty irrigation water and was itching him terribly, but he didn't want to seem weak in front of Amanda. He also didn't want to be sprayed with house water from a hose, because even though the day was hot, house water was cold, even colder than irrigation water that was slightly warmed by the sun while it traveled through the ditches.

"Are you sure?" she asked, truly concerned.

"Yeah, I'm fine," he said, resisting the urge to continue scratching.

Amanda stood up and began to walk the rest of the way to the picnic table where they had left their bikes. Jamie followed her.

"Do you ever float down irrigation ditches in an inner tube?" Amanda asked, once they were back at the picnic table. She plopped down on the bench. Jamie sat across from her, self-conscious, since the little boy was still eyeing them.

"Are you serious?" Jamie asked. "That would be dangerous."

"Yeah, I know, and I would never do it," Amanda said. "My parents would never let me, especially up on the hill. The ditches are bigger, and the water is much deeper than this one. But it's weird, sometimes when I go to Mindy's house, her mom tells us to get inner tubes from their garage and take them up the hill to the irrigation ditch that's about a block from her house, and we float in them, down to where the ditch goes under the road.

"It's so weird, because her mom is usually so strict, like when we want to go downtown, she always tells us, 'Why don't you sit down and read a book?' So, we have to do what she tells us. I've only floated the ditch a couple times with Mindy, but she does it all the time in the summer when it gets hot."

Jamie watched as Amanda told the story, using her hands to exaggerate the expressions on her face.

"It's really kind of scary, because, for one thing, the inner tubes are so big, they just barely fit in the ditch and they keep hitting the sides, so you bounce from one side to the other. The really scary part is, if you don't stop and get out in time, you'll go under the road, and I don't know exactly where it comes out, you know, how far you would go under the road. What if the water gets deeper, or the space between the water and the under part of the road gets smaller?

"When I went with Mindy, I jumped out of the inner tube about a half a block before we got to where it goes under the road. The water was kind of swift, but it wasn't really deep, maybe three feet. Last time, the inner tube just kept on going when I jumped out, and there I was, standing in the middle of the irrigation ditch and my inner tube was floating away. I tried to run after it, but how can you run in the water? I couldn't catch the inner tube. So, I climbed out and started running along the ditch. When I finally caught up to the inner tube, it was almost to the place where the ditch goes under the road, and I couldn't grab it, so I jumped inside it; I mean, into the water, inside the inner tube. I was a little bit scared. Mindy was a ways behind me and when she caught up to me, she just stood up and got out, like it was the easiest thing in the world. She was laughing pretty hard at me."

"So, you and her have been friends for a long time?" he asked. He still couldn't figure out why, since the two girls were so different.

"Yeah, ever since she moved here in the fourth grade," Amanda said. "She sat by me, even though her last name starts with an S and mine starts with F, but one girl left just two days before Mindy came to our classroom, and the other girl sat right across from me, so, instead of having all the students who were alphabetical after the other girl move one desk ahead, the teacher just put Mindy in the old girl's desk, right across from me.

"Right after she started in our classroom, we were taking a quiz about California, and she just moved here from California, so I thought she would know everything about it. I looked over at her and I saw her cheating. She had a piece of paper between her legs and she was copying answers from it. She saw me and knew that I saw her, and I didn't tell on her, and we became friends after that."

"So... you became friends with her because she was a cheater?" Jamie asked. That didn't make any more sense than why they were friends now.

"No, we became friends because she trusted me," Amanda said. "Then I found out that she is really smart, but she was just nervous because we had a test right after she got here. She never cheated after that."

"You mean, you never saw her cheating after that," Jamie said.

"No, I mean that she never cheated after that," Amanda said. "She was really scared that she was going to get caught, so she made a pinky promise to me that she would never cheat again. And I believed her. She would never break a pinky promise."

"What's a pinky promise?" Jamie asked, smiling that silly smile. It sounded very strange.

"Well, it's what you have to make to me right now," Amanda said, "because I just told you a secret about Mindy, and I've never, ever told anyone that before, and you have to promise me that you will never tell anyone that I told you. Or that she cheated on that quiz in the fourth grade."

"Okay, I promise," he said. He didn't know anyone who would be interested in this information anyway.

"No, you have to do it like this," Amanda said. "Put up your pinky finger, your right pinky." She put up hers to demonstrate, and Jamie did the same.

"Now," she said, "we hook them around each other like this, no, bend it a little, no, loop it around mine. Haven't you ever done this before?"

"I haven't ever even heard of a pinky promise before," Jamie said, grinning and feeling goofy. He tried to make his expression look serious. "I promise."

"Okay, now that we have our pinkies together like this," she said, tightly gripping his pinky with hers, "you have to promise that you won't tell anyone about Mindy cheating on the quiz when we were in the fourth grade."

"Okay, I promise I won't tell anyone about Mindy cheating on the quiz when we were in the fourth grade," Jamie repeated.

"No, when WE were in the fourth grade," Amanda corrected.

"No, when WE were in the fourth grade," Jamie repeated.

"Oh, that's right," she said, "you were in the fourth grade at the same time we were in the fourth grade! You were just in a different fourth grade at a different school."

"Yep!" Jamie said. He was enjoying holding her pinky with his pinky, and he wondered if he would ever have the courage to actually hold her hand. He kept smiling, not wanting to let her pinky get away from his pinky.

JAMIE
Now

Jamie slipped into Amanda's room as soon as he saw she that she was alone. He examined her face closely – no change in her condition. He had to talk to her, had to make her realize they were meant to be together, fate had finally brought them together, so when she woke up, she would know. If he spoke it to her, out loud, she would hear in her subconscience. He very gently touched her hand.

"Guess what, Amanda," he began, swallowing hard. "I live in that castle, the one on Yakima Avenue that you love. I wanted to tell you all about it, but it was hard for me to talk about it. Yes, it's a beautiful structure, but it hasn't been a home to me in a long time. My mom –" he kind of choked when he mentioned her "– went away when I was in kindergarten, and it became a cold, empty place to live. When my dad died, he left it to my sisters and me, but they didn't want to live in Yakima, so it's all mine.

"Amanda, it could be ours. No, it should be ours, mine and yours. With you there, it would be a home. Your light would give it life. With you there, I would feel like a king, and you would be my queen; the queen of my castle. As soon as you wake up, the castle is yours; I mean, ours.

"Don't you think it's strange how all our circumstances finally brought us together? Now that I look back, I can see how all our roads, from way back there, brought us here."

NICHOLAS
Then

"I won't be travelling as much for my job, so you can come and live with me in Montana," Nick's dad said. "Not just for the summer, but for good. Just like I always promised you."

Nick couldn't believe what he was hearing. When he had first moved in with his grandparents, he had wanted nothing more than to go back home to Montana and live with his dad. He hadn't really thought it would ever happen, though, and now that it was happening, he was afraid – afraid of losing Mandy. He was only ten years old, but he knew true love when he felt it, and he truly loved Mandy. He knew she loved him, too. It was their destiny to grow up together and get married and grow old together, the same way his grandparents had. He had loved her ever since second grade. He couldn't just leave her.

"You mean, go to school there, and everything?" he asked, his breath catching in his throat.

"Yes. They have a great school there, smaller than Gilbert, but you will like it. I think you might be ahead of your class there, academically, but you will get along well there. You already know Jack and Kirby and Donald, our neighbors. They will be in your class. And there's a cute new girl who just moved in down the street."

"I have..." he began, then trailed off. He hadn't told his dad about Mandy. He couldn't tell him. He wouldn't understand. Ever since his mother had died, his dad learned to live without love, or without that kind of love. His dad loved only his mother, the memory of his mother, and he put all his energy and focus into his work. He loved Nick, too, and worked hard to make the best life he could for his son.

"We can stay here a few more days, until school is out, and then we'll pack up your stuff and move you home, where you belong." His dad's word was final. He wasn't intending to be heartless or to hurt Nick – he had no idea about Nick's attachment to this town. He had no idea that Nick was in love with Mandy. His dad looked so happy, Nick didn't dare tell him about her.

Nick's heart was heavy. He couldn't just disappear from Mandy's life. He couldn't just tell her in a letter that he was leaving for good.

His dad must have sensed that something was wrong. "If things don't work out, if you are too far ahead of your class in school, or if I have to start traveling again, you can come back here and live with Grandma and Grandpa again. Let's give it a year, one school year, and see what happens."

Nick suddenly had a sliver of hope. Maybe being apart from each other for one year would help their love grow stronger. He could come back, he would come back. In the meantime, they could write to each other. However, he had to tell her, face-to-face, that he was leaving.

"Did you tell Grandma and Grandpa?" he asked, suddenly feeling sorry for them. They had raised Nick as their own, since he was two years old, with his dad just taking him during vacation times. What would they do without him?

"Yes, we talked about it already," his dad said. "They agree that it's best for us to be together, to live together, now that I have things at work straightened out. And now you are older. You can do a lot of things to take care of yourself. Grandma and Grandpa knew you were only staying with them temporarily, until I could be home more."

Most of his life hardly seemed to Nick to be temporary. His life and his friends were all here, in Yakima. His love was here.

"Your grandmother told me that you have a little girl-friend," his dad said, out of the blue.

Nick felt himself turning all shades of red. This was not the direction this conversation should be going! He couldn't talk to his dad about Mandy. He would never understand. Really, he called her a 'little girlfriend!' Mandy was so much more to him than that! She was the love of his life!

"Do you want to go over to her house so you can tell her you are moving away?" his dad suggested. "Do you know where she lives?"

Nick nodded. Of course he knew where she lived! He had never been inside her house, but he had become friends with Brad Martin just because he lived around the corner from Mandy. He had watched her riding her bike and playing with her friends from Brad's bedroom window. Nick had walked home with Brad so he could walk behind Mandy and her friends, all the way home. He had seen her walk into her own house. He had often imagined himself walking up to her door, knocking, and being invited into that very house. Yes, he knew exactly where she lived.

"Why don't we go over there now?" his dad suggested.

"Right now?" Nick asked, feeling his heart rate begin to increase.

"There's no time like the present," his dad said.

"Maybe she isn't home now," Nick said, in an attempt to get his thoughts together, and what he was going to say to her.

"There's only one way to find out," his dad said. "Come on."

As their car neared Mandy's street, Nick decided he wouldn't say anything to Mandy. He would let his dad tell it. Nick would just stand there next to him and watch Mandy's reaction. He didn't have to say anything. How could he?

"That's it," he said, pointing to Mandy's house. Two cars were in the carport. That meant her mom and dad were both at home.

His dad stopped the car in front of the house. Nick followed his dad up the sidewalk, dreading the scene that was about to happen. His dad rang the doorbell.

Mandy's mother came to the door.

"May I help you?" she asked, looking at his dad. Then she noticed Nick standing behind him.

"Well, Nick," she said sweetly, "it's so nice to see you. Come on in." She opened the door wide and stepped out of the way so they could enter.

"This is my dad, Joe Robbins," Nick said, in a feeble attempt at an introduction. He and his dad went into Mandy's house, which had the feeling of a wonderful home, a perfect home. The furniture was modern, yet spotless, and real paintings hung on the walls. This wasn't like his grandparents' home, all muted green and flowery, the way old people liked their homes to be. This was a modern home where a complete family lived.

"I am Mandy's mother, Della Foster," she said, extending her hand, "and this is my husband, Joe."

Nick had known both of their dads were named Joe, but it seemed strange for both Joes to be in the same room at the same time; or even in the same state. Mandy's dad reached in to shake his dad's hand, the two Joes finally meeting.

"Mandy!" her mother called. "Someone is here to see you!"

"Coming!" was the reply from upstairs. Nick felt like an intruder into Mandy's privacy. She was probably in her own bedroom, after all!

"I assume you are here to see Mandy?" her mother asked. "Can I get you something to drink, some coffee or anything?"

"No, we can't stay long," his dad said, somewhat disappointing Nick. He thought they could stay all evening, maybe have dinner and play Monopoly later.

He heard footsteps on the stairs and Mandy came around the corner. She looked surprised when she saw Nick.

"Hi," she said shyly, looking from Nick to his dad with a question mark on her face.

"Have a seat," her mother said, and the men obediently sat, her dad in the big chair, his dad on the sofa. Nick plopped down beside his dad while Mandy stood in the doorway.

"I have heard from my mother that Nick and your daughter are friends," his dad said.

Nick saw Mandy blush, her face turning a deep red, as she glanced at him then looked down at the floor. His face was burning up. His dad really knew how to get to the heart of the matter in a hurry, didn't he?

"Mandy has been liking Nick for a couple of years now, I think," her mother said.

"Mom!" Mandy whispered, not looking at anyone.

"You have a fine boy there, Joe," her dad said.

"Well, thank you, Joe," his dad said.

"Would you like to stay for dinner?" her mother asked. "Mandy can set two more places. We can eat in the dining room."

Nick watched out of the corner of his eye – he couldn't be caught looking straight at her. Mandy's face lit up with anticipation, as if this were a social visit, a chance for the two families to get to know each other.

"No, thank you," his dad said. "I appreciate the invitation, but we came because we have something to tell you."

"Is everything all right?" Mandy asked, a worried look crossing her face. "Are your grandmother and grandfather all right?" She was now looking directly at Nick, but he pressed his lips together and looked down, avoiding her eyes.

"Everyone is fine," his dad said. "We wanted to come and tell you in person about our plans."

Nick glanced at Mandy and her parents as they looked at each other with question marks on their faces. His dad nudged him, but Nick was not going to be the one to break the news. He stared at the blue and green pattern of the carpet as if it were suddenly very interesting.

"You know that Nick has been coming to stay with me in Montana during the summers," his dad began.

"Where in Montana do you live?" Mandy's mother asked. "We lived just outside of Butte when I was in the second grade."

"Great Falls," his dad said.

"Oh, you're farther north," she said, nodding.

"Yes," his dad confirmed.

"You must really get the snow in the winter," Mandy's dad added.

"Yes, we can get quite a lot of snow at times," his dad agreed. Why didn't he just get to the point? They were just wasting time with idle conversation when something so important had to be said.

"We had a lot of snow in Butte," her mom said, "but they get a lot more in Great Falls."

"What do you do there?" her dad asked. "For a living, I mean."

"I work for Trident," his dad said. "I'm one of their corporate lawyers. They were having me travel all over the country much of the year, but now they've given me an opportunity to stay in one place. That's why we are here now. Nick is going to stay with me, not just through the summer, but through the school year. He's moving to Great Falls to live with me full time."

Nick saw Mandy's face fall, and with it, his heart fell. Her eyes had such a look of hurt in them – but only for a second. She tipped her head back and set her jaw. He thought she was doing that to prevent herself from crying.

"Well, that will be nice for you," her mom said. "You must miss him terribly when he's here and you are there."

The conversation turned to a blur, as they began discussing her dad's new barbecue and the plan for them to get a new car. Nick's head was swimming. Mandy's deep brown eyes had a glaze over them, an unseeing look, like she was staring straight ahead.

"It's hot in here," she said suddenly, jumping to her feet. "Want to go out to the patio?" she asked him.

"Yes, go on outside for a few minutes," her mother insisted, as the grown-ups headed for the carport.

Nick followed Mandy through the kitchen to the patio, where it was nice and shady and cool.

"I don't want to leave," he said quietly.

Mandy looked at him but didn't say anything. He really didn't want her to start crying.

"I'll probably be back next year," he said hopefully.

"That's good," she said, almost under her breath. She

was looking out at the back yard. She had to understand that this was as hard for him as it was for her.

"Come over here," he said, slightly taking her hand, guiding her behind the big apple tree. He didn't want to lose her, not now, not while he was gone for a year, not ever.

She went along with him.

"While I am there, I might meet some other girls," he began, rambling, not knowing what he was going to say. "I want you to be mine, even while I am gone."

"We can write to each other," she said, "like we did last summer when you were there."

"This will be for a whole year," he said. "I'm going to be gone for a whole year, for all of fifth grade. I might come back for sixth grade, but only if I have someone to come back to."

"I haven't ever had any other boyfriend," she said.

"And I haven't had another girlfriend," he said, "and I don't want one."

She gave him a little smile.

"We have to make sure…" he didn't know what he really wanted to say, but right now, he knew what he wanted to do. "Let us pledge ourselves to each other and seal it with a kiss."

She looked at him doubtfully.

"If I kiss you, I will know, and you will know, that you are the only girl for me."

"I don't know if we should…"

She hesitated, pressing her lips together, revealing those dimples.

"But we can't tell anyone," he added. "It will be our secret. We can't tell ANYONE. Can you keep a secret like that?"

127

She nodded.

"We will be proving that we don't need anyone else," he said. "But only if you agree. I don't want you to do anything you don't want to do."

"I want to," she said, looking up at him.

He closed his eyes and leaned over to her, his lips brushing hers. He hadn't ever kissed anyone but his grand-mother, but this was not the same. He pressed his lips harder on hers and held them there for a few seconds. She pulled away, but he kissed her again. She didn't pull away this time, not for a while, and when they finished, they looked into each other's eyes.

"Now you are mine," he whispered.

She smiled sweetly at him and nodded, not taking her eyes from his.

MANDY

I am walking across the grade school playground toward my car. It is already getting dark and it's not even four o'clock. In December, our days are so short; or should I say, our daylight hours are so short. I have the paperwork I need, and my heart is so heavy. I won't be coming back to this school for quite some time.

A lady approaches me and smiles at me, looking at my growing belly.

"You are so blessed," she says, running up the steps and passing me.

I don't feel blessed. Yes, we have a child on the way, but we are about to have a funeral for my twin 10-year-old sons. I would rather have my boys back, the two boys I already know and love so well, than to have this unknown child.

When I get to the car, I sit down, and I break down and cry for the loss of my sons.

EARNEST
Now

Although he still had not made the effort to sell the two cars his mother had owned, Earnest could not drive either of them to Seattle. He prayed to God and asked Him to make a way for him to get to the hospital so he could see Sister Peoples. She had been there for more than a week, and she was still in a coma. Now that he knew where she was, he called the hospital daily to check on her condition.

One morning he woke up with the answer to his prayer. God gave him the strength to make the trip by bus. It took prayer as well as planning to discover the way he would have to go. First, he would have to take the city bus to the downtown station. There he would catch the interstate bus to Portland. Then he would catch the Portland city bus to the Greyhound station and from there, ride to Seattle. In Seattle, he would catch the city bus that would take him up near the hospital.

He researched and planned his route by using the Internet, so he had it in his mind, as well as printed on paper. The difficult part would be putting the plan into action. Memorizing it was not going to get him there. He tried to not think about the body odors of the other people on the bus, the germs on the seats and in the air on the bus, the disgusting acts that could occur on a bus. After staying up all night worrying about the endless possibilities of problems he could have, he fixed himself a lunch to take with him, and a dinner, then he filled his backpack with food he could eat without having to approach a fast food restaurant or vending machine, grabbed his Bible, and forced his feet to walk him to the city bus stop. He prayed with every step, and when he sat on the bench to wait for the bus, he buried his face in his Bible. He began to read and re-read scripture passages to give himself strength – or, no, to get strength from God for this urgent task that he had to keep telling himself was not impossible.

The ride on the first bus was the most difficult. When the door opened at the front of the bus, he knew that was where he was to enter, but he didn't know where to pay his fare or, once he figured it out, where he should sit. He could not sit in a seat with someone else, so he moved back until he found an empty seat, nearly stumbling when the bus lurched forward. His heart was pounding so hard as he looked down, not meeting the eyes of any of the other passengers, who were surely laughing at him. He was sweating but dared not remove his coat. He couldn't take a chance that he might leave it on the bus. He did not want to look out the windows, so he again opened his Bible, but he just stared at the pages, not able to even read one word. When the bus stopped at the transit center downtown, he found where to catch the inter-state bus and waited.

The rest of the trip was slightly easier, as he kept his mind on the goal – to see Sister Peoples – and his eyes in his Bible, from bus to bus, from city to city, until that evening when he finally stepped out of the last bus and looked up at the great hospital in front of him. He felt a huge sense of relief, as well as a little bit of satisfaction of achieving his goal. He was here! The rest would be easy.

EARNEST
Then

"What took you so long?" Earnest's mother asked, as she put her car in reverse to back out of his driveway. "What have you been doing all this time? Did you have to keep me out here waiting like this? I have been waiting here for you for at least three minutes, and you know it is not good to keep a car like this running, just sitting in one place, without moving, not to mention all the gas I have been wasting. You really need to learn to be more considerate of your elders, and especially of me, your mother. I'm the only mother you'll ever have, and you really need to show me more respect. I have been taking care of you all of your life, and this is how you repay me? Maybe you can start buying the gas for my car."

"I'm sorry, Mother," Earnest said, trying to get his seat belt buckled before she started driving. He felt like he was always apologizing to her for things that were not really his fault. She had arrived nearly ten minutes early, and he didn't even know she was waiting in the driveway until she honked the horn five times. He hoped his neighbors would not be upset by his mother's neighborhood rudeness. He wanted to duck down in his seat in case any of them were looking out the window, so they wouldn't see him.

"I know this is your first time going to choir rehearsal," his mother said, "so I just want you to be aware of a few things, or, should I say, a few people in the choir. Some of the choir members are very sensitive about their voices, so don't criticize anyone, even the ones who can't carry a tune in a bucket. Sister Josene will need to be praised every few minutes or she will think she is being ignored. She thinks she is the diva of the choir, but we don't have a diva in this choir. I am the only one, praise God, who is ever given solos, so some of the sisters may act like they are a little jealous of me, but I have to use what the good Lord has given me, the gift He has bestowed upon me, for His glory, so I don't apologize for what I have. Sister Magda is always off key and off tempo, but her voice is so faint, we can drown her out if we sing loud enough. Sister Marta can carry a tune, but her voice sounds like a little girl, so we have to make sure we can cover it with our voices. I am so glad you have a beautiful singing voice, bless the Lord. He has not been stingy with vocal talent in our family."

Earnest was beginning to think coming to choir rehearsal was a mistake. He didn't like the way his mother, the self-proclaimed holy saint, berated the other members of the church, as if she were the only one who took the time to read the Bible, enough time so that she could beat others over the head with her knowledge. He knew she was expecting him to join the choir, but now he was feeling like he might be coming just this one time, and then make an excuse for not joining the choir.

His mother pulled into the parking lot at the church and parked in one of the handicap spaces.

"Mom, this is a handicap space," Earnest said. Maybe she hadn't noticed. She usually kept her car parked in her own garage at her house, across the street from the church, and walked across the street. "Are you sure you should be parking here? Maybe you should save it for someone who is really handicapped."

"I am the oldest member of the choir, chronologically speaking, as well as spiritually speaking," she snipped, "and

I deserve to be able to park the closest to the door. We don't have any handicapped people in our choir."

"If you want to park closest to the door, why don't you park in the pastor's space?" he asked, aware that he should be speaking to her with a tone more becoming a Christian, but she just made him so angry sometimes. He took a deep breath and decided right then and there that he would not be coming to choir rehearsal with her again.

"Oh, I can't park in the pastor's space," she said, as if he had been serious. "Sister Peoples has to park there, even though she's usually late for choir rehearsal. I can forgive her, though, since she has to deal with those two boys of hers all the time. At least she makes an effort and her singing voice is not half bad, if you know what I mean."

Earnest didn't hear a word she said after 'Sister Peoples has to park there.' He didn't know she was coming to choir rehearsal! He immediately reversed his earlier decision to not join the choir. After all, he had to give it a try, didn't he, to see if he liked it or not. He couldn't make a decision just like that, before he even went inside the building.

He and his mother were the first to arrive at church that evening, about fifteen or twenty minutes early. His mother unlocked the front door with her key. As soon as she opened the door, she turned to her son.

"Earnest, Dear, can you prop the doors open?" she asked sweetly, having somehow transformed into a loving mother at the house of God. "It is so stuffy in here. Let some of that sweet springtime evening air inside."

Earnest did as his mother asked, his heart skipping beats. He didn't know why he was feeling so excited to see Sister Peoples this evening. He had been riding to church in her car with her on Sundays, and that was always very nice. She usually did most of the talking, since he felt so shy around her, well, he was shy around everyone; and also, she was so sweet to him all the time. She was patient with him when he was a little bit late, and she spoke to her boys in a loving voice as well.

Oh, he had heard her sing! She often sang in the car, using some kind of master plan to keep her boys from arguing. They would join in the singing and forget all about their bickering. She did have a nice voice. Why didn't it occur to him that she might be in the choir?

He now realized why he hadn't thought about it. He had always looked up to her, as if she were some special member of the church, being the pastor's wife and all. Yet, she behaved just the same as any other true Christian, with a quiet and calm demeanor and with patience and love. She always treated everyone with patience and love, even the ones who criticized her behind her back. He did feel sorry for her, because no matter what she did, she was constantly being scrutinized by the members of the congregation, usually the other women, who made up about eighty percent of the members. He heard them talking about her, even though he didn't acknowledge their evil conversation. A woman could be sitting in church with the most raggedy jeans and she would say that Sister Peoples was overdressed and trying to show off. Another woman who was dressed in clothes she might wear to an evening date of dinner and dancing would say that Sister Peoples wasn't dressed up enough to honor God. Some of the women said that Sister Peoples shouldn't be so involved in everything at church, and other women said she didn't do enough for the church, like, she should make new curtains for all the windows by hand, or she should organize more potlucks and dinners for the church, as well as cook and bring all the food so the members could eat a free meal without having to do any work. He was sure she didn't know any of this trash talk about her, because, if she did, how could she be so nice to everyone all the time?

Earnest sat in one of the back pews and admired the beauty of the sanctuary. The stained-glass windows on the south side let the sunlight stream through, casting multi-colored shadows all around the room. The deep blue seats on the pews richly complemented the dark cherry wood. The large cross at the front of the sanctuary, behind the pulpit, drew his eyes and he stared at it. A sense of complete peace and surrender washed over him like a wave. He closed his eyes and silently prayed, feeling like he was in direct contact with God. He prayed first for his mother, who needed a measure of patience for people, along with a spoonful of understanding. He then prayed for Sister Peoples and her family, acknowledging that only God knew exactly what they needed. He then prayed for himself, asking only that God's will would be done in his life, every moment of every day. He began mentally going down his prayer list, asking the Lord to bless each person as he thought of his or her name, in the way that each one needed most. He felt like he was floating a few inches above the pew, and going higher, in contact with God.

"Good evening!" Sister People's cheerful voice said.

Earnest opened his eyes, almost surprised to discover that he was still sitting in the pew at church. He had felt as if he were about halfway to heaven.

"Hi, Brother Earnest," one of the twins said, coming over to sit beside him. Earnest could never tell which one was which.

"Hello," he said, always a safe answer.

"Yeah, hell IS low!" the other twin said, pointing to the floor. "All the way down there!"

"Caleb!" the first twin said, who Earnest now knew was Joshua. "We're at church! You know we are not supposed to say the H-E-double-hockey-stick word!"

"Brother Earnest said it first!" Caleb accused.

"Boys, come on back to the Sunday School room," their mother said, firmly but kindly. "I have some posters I need you to color for the revival next week." She reached out both hands to her boys and smiled at Earnest. "How are you doing this evening, Brother Earnest?"

"I'm fine," he answered. He could never think of what to say to her! He should not feel flustered around another man's wife, especially his pastor's wife. She was just being nice to him, like she was nice to everyone, he told himself. She was really pretty, though, and he did like her, as a friend, just a friend. She was a very nice friend to everyone at this church, and he was included in that group.

"I'll be right back, as soon as I get these boys started on a project in the Sunday School room," she said, following them down the hall. "This will keep them busy for a while."

"Mom, can we use the markers?" one of the twins asked. Earnest had already lost track of which one was which. "I don't want to use crayons. They are for babies."

"Yes, you can use the markers," she assured her boys, as the three of them left the sanctuary.

Earnest's mother came out of one of the back rooms carrying the choir song books.

"Did I hear voices?" she asked, looking around the empty room.

"Yes," Earnest replied. "Sister Peoples and her two twins are here, in the Sunday School room. She is getting them set up with a project."

"Earnest, you don't need to say 'two twins,' really!" his mother said sternly, as if she were correcting a child instead of a grown man. "The word 'twins' means two identical children. There would not be three twins or five twins."

"Yes, ma'am," he said, absorbing his mother's criticism.

"Well, I am surprised that she is here early," his mother continued. "She is almost always late for choir rehearsal, even if it's only a few minutes. I bet you I can count on one hand the number of times she has been on time. I am actually very surprised." She put her purse and her shawl on her spot on the first pew and went up to her place in the choir stand. She began to flip through a song book.

"Good evening, Sister Miller," Sister Peoples said with a smile.

"Good evening, Sister Peoples," his mother replied. He winced in anticipation of what would come out of her mouth next. A bat flying out would be preferable to just about anything she might say. "It's so good of you to be on time, for once. Come on up here and give me a hug," she commanded.

Sister Peoples walked toward the choir stand.

"And not one of those side-hugs, like you usually give me," his mother instructed. "Give me a REAL hug, like you mean it; like you are happy to see me. You young people need to show respect to your elders at all times."

Sister Peoples went up and gave her a proper hug. Earnest saw his mother smile with delight as she received her hug, the same smile she always made when she got her way.

"I don't know where everyone else is," his mother said, when the hug was finished, "but I was just looking through the song book and selecting some hymns for us to sing during the revival next week."

"That's great," Sister Peoples acknowledged. "It is almost 6:00 now. Why don't we say a prayer and share a few minutes of testimony while we are waiting for the others to arrive?"

Before his mother could object to this lovely idea, Earnest chimed in. "Yes, let's do that."

His mother gave him that look, the look that said he was out of line, but she was too late to overrule Sister Peoples now.

"Well, all right," his mother agreed. "That is a good idea," she added, as if it were her idea.

"Brother Earnest, will you give us an opening prayer?" Sister Peoples asked. She closed her eyes and bowed her head.

He was stunned, on the spot, but he had to respond. Think, think, think! of how to say a public prayer, he thought. "Our Heavenly Father, bless us for this session and that it may bring glory to You. Amen." He was sweating heavily. He would not be able to remove his jacket now.

"Is that all?" his mother asked.

"That's all we need," Sister Peoples assured them. "Sister Miller, would you like to testify first?"

"Are you saying, 'age before beauty,' Sister Peoples?" his mother asked. Earnest didn't know if she were teasing or not. "I will let you two young people testify first."

Only his mother could refer to them (he thought, he wasn't sure how old Sister Peoples was) as 'young people' and get away with it. He could imagine the remarks of the real young people of the church if they had heard her say that.

"Brother Earnest?" Sister Peoples said. He would have preferred for her to go first, but he had learned to be obedient.

"I just want to thank God, the Father, for all good things," he began, "and I thank His Son, Jesus Christ, for all He has done for us. Just to show you how good God is, and how He always provides for His children, last week I got a letter

139

from the state, telling me that my benefits were going to be cut off at the end of this month. I got down on my knees and prayed and asked God to continue to take care of me, and I reminded Him that Jesus said He would take care of me just like He takes care of the sparrows. I asked God that His will would be done in my life. And I didn't worry about it. I didn't call the office and demand that they reinstate my benefits or anything. I just put it in God's hands, and I trusted Him to take care of me, the way He promised He always will.

"Well, anyway, to make a long story short, today in the mail I got another letter from the state. This letter said that the other letter I received last week was a mistake! This letter told me to ignore the previous letter, and not to worry, because my benefits were going to continue. And not only that, this letter stated that I am going to get a raise of forty-nine dollars per month! Now, you tell me, isn't God good?"

"Praise God!" Sister Peoples and his mother said, at the same time. Earnest was really sweating now. He hoped his deodorant was working.

"Go ahead and testify, Sister Peoples," his mother prompted.

"I thank God for being here tonight," she said, "and for each of you who are here with me, and blessings upon those who are making their way here, and for those who would like to be here tonight and can't make it. I was just so blessed today during my Bible study time, as we were studying in the book of Genesis. I have really fallen in love with the book of Genesis, and we are getting close to the end, and, to tell the truth, I'm not ready to move on! I am really loving it, and I would love to just stay here for another month or so. Oh, I didn't mention, I am studying with Thru the Bible Radio, the five-year Bible Study course. Every day, well, five days a week, we study the Bible with our radio teacher, Dr. J. Vernon McGee. He is, without a doubt, a Spirit-filled teacher, and he brings out all the spiritual truths that a person can only get when he is really studying and praying as while he studies."

"Didn't Dr. McGee die?" Earnest's mother asked.

"Yes, he died in 1988," Sister Peoples said, "but his teaching of the Bible is timeless. It is still relevant for us today. He did so much research, and he prayed and studied to get the spiritual meaning out of every verse of the entire Bible. Did you know that he could find Jesus in every chapter of the Old Testament, and in almost every verse?"

"I don't see how that is possible," Earnest's mother said, "especially for someone who is dead, and has been dead for all these years."

"It's like the blood of Abel," Sister Peoples said, "though he be dead, yet he speaketh. It's because he taught the Word of God, and it doesn't change. He wasn't teaching a philosophy or a way of life or a method of living. He taught the Bible. Heaven and earth will pass away, but the Word of God, the Bible, will stand forever. If you want to listen for yourself, the program is on the Christian radio station at 7:30 in the morning, 6:30 in the evening and 10:30 at night. It's nice, they give you so many options to listen."

"So, that's your testimony?" his mother asked, as if she were expecting something so fantastic. Earnest tuned her out, as he so often did, and he memorized those times Sister Peoples had just mentioned. He could go through the Bible with the radio program, and it would be almost as if he were studying along with Sister Peoples. As an added benefit, he would be guided as he learned the Bible. He made two decisions at that very moment: he would start tomorrow studying the Bible daily with the late Dr. McGee, and tonight he would officially join the choir.

MANDY

We are at a hotel, but we need to get ready to go. I have so many things to pack; I can't forget anything. My husband and our boys are lounging around, waiting for me to do everything so we can leave on time. I am folding clothes, trying to fit them in the suitcase, but as soon as I close the suitcase, I see a few more items on the dresser. I gather them in my hands, so many little items, now I can't open the suitcase again without dropping something.

The boys are watching TV, so I ask them to please help me. They move out of the room with my husband, the TV is making irritating noises, I am running out of time, and I have to make sure we don't leave anything behind.

I am not a juggler! Things are slipping away, and I can't fix it. My husband and sons have slipped out of the room, and I am left with these useless items which were, at one time, so important.

I drop everything to join them, but as I leave the room, the door behind me has closed and locked, and I don't have the key. I don't care about getting back inside the room – now the door isn't even there anymore.

The hallway is empty. My family has vanished. I feel like I will never see them again, and my heart is breaking.

JAMIE
Then

Jamie rode his bike to Franklin Park, just to get out of the empty house. The only person even close to the house was Raul, the gardener, but he didn't speak English.

Jamie rode down the grassy terraces, gaining speed with each one, making his way to a big shady evergreen tree near the pool. He noticed that the swimming session had just ended, and lots of kids were being picked up in the parking lot by their parents. He even saw that pervert guy, the man Amanda had pointed out several times near Wilson Junior High. The man often sat in his car and watched the scantily clad girls as they were coming out of the school building. He wasn't there to pick up children of his own, but he just sat there, watching the girls. Now the pervert guy was watching two skinny girls in bikinis as they bounded from the pool locker room to a waiting car in the parking lot. As soon as they got in their car, Jamie watched the pervert guy as his attention turned to a group of three girls in their swimming suits, who were standing on the curb, waiting for their ride.

When Jamie got to the evergreen tree, he discovered a couple was lying on the grass, making out beneath it. He rode his bike over towards the old museum, which had been closed down for quite some time. He was surprised to see Amanda standing in the shade behind the building. He rode over to her and stopped.

"Hey, Jamie!" she said excitedly. She looked like she was really happy to see him. "What are you doing here?"

"Nothing," he said. "Just riding my bike. What are you doing?"

"We just finished swimming, Mindy and I, and we are waiting for her mother to pick us up," Amanda said. "She's always about an hour late picking us up."

"Where is she?" Jamie asked, looking around the huge park.

"Who knows?" Amanda replied. "I just know she is always late, and then she gets all mad and she acts like it's our fault."

"No, I mean where is Mindy?" Jamie clarified, smiling at Amanda's answer.

"Oh, don't tell anyone, but she's in there," Amanda said, pointing to the men's bathroom door, in the basement of the museum. "They always lock the women's bathroom door, but they don't lock the men's," she explained. "I'm standing guard so no men will go in while she's in there."

"Why didn't she just go over at the pool?" Jamie asked, a very logical question.

"Oh, in the girls' locker room at the pool, the stalls don't have doors, and she doesn't want anyone to see her go," Amanda said, as if that were a logical answer.

"Oh, I see," Jamie said, smiling shyly, amazed at his incredible luck in running into Amanda today.

A big, fat black and white cat came around the corner of the museum and wandered by Jamie and Amanda. It paused and looked at them for a second before continuing to walk across the park.

"That looks a little like our cat, only Tiffiny isn't so fat," Amanda said, watching the cat. Jamie was watching Amanda. "Well, she is kind of fat, but don't tell her. She thinks she is just big boned. I really love cats."

144

"Your cat is named Tiffiny?" Jamie asked. "That's my sister's name."

"You have a sister named Tiffiny?" Amanda asked.

"Yeah, and one named Misty," he said. "My other sister is named Misty. They are really old, more than ten years older than us, and they both moved out a long time ago." He looked at the grass beneath his bike as he spoke. He cast his eyes across the park to where a group of older kids were drinking beer behind a tree, hoping Amanda wouldn't press for any details, almost wishing he hadn't said anything. He wouldn't have mentioned his family if she hadn't said her cat had the same name as his sister.

Amanda seemed to sense that his home life was a sensitive subject, and she quickly changed the subject.

"We used to have a dog named Alice," she said.

"You had a dog named Alice?" he laughed.

"Yeah, I know, it's a dumb name for a dog," she said. "We didn't name her that, she already had that name when we got her. I would never name a dog Alice. I wanted to change her name to Blackie, because she was all black, but my mom said no, she had to keep the name of Alice. I didn't think she looked like an Alice, so I secretly called her Blackie."

"What kind of dog was she?" he asked, sitting back on the seat of his bike, finally releasing the handlebars.

"I'm not sure. She was some mixed breed, but she was all black, kind of small, smaller than a Lassie dog, but bigger than a Pomeranian. She had a long, bushy tail. I didn't really know what to do with her."

"What happened to her?" he asked.

"We got her when I was in the second grade, and, like I said, I didn't know what to do with her. I played with her a little, and when I was walking home from school, I always called her when I got to the end of our street, so she could walk the rest of the way home with me. Sometimes she came when I called her, and sometimes she didn't. A few days in a row, she didn't come, and I didn't really think about her that much. I mean, Alice-Blackie didn't sleep on my bed, like Tiffiny does, and I didn't feed her, and I didn't know how to play with her or anything. So, anyway, one day when I was walking home with Erin, my next-door-neighbor, I called for Blackie, and she didn't come. Erin told me that her mother told her, but she wasn't supposed to tell me, that my mom gave Alice away to some of her other friends about a week before that.

"I couldn't believe it, so I ran home, calling Blackie and Alice all the way. When I got to the house, I asked my mom if she had seen her. My mom told me that she gave Alice to a family we know that has four kids, because I didn't ever play with her. She said that if I had asked what had happened to her sooner, or missed her sooner, she would have gone to get her back, but since I didn't miss her for a whole week, I wasn't ready to have a dog. I cried a little for her, but really, I didn't miss her. About a week later, she got hit by a car, because the people my mom gave her to live on a busy street. I told my mom it was her fault for giving her away and she said it was my fault for ignoring her. Then, we didn't have any pets for a long time, until I was in sixth grade, one time, I was sick for about two weeks, and then my mom brought home a little, tiny kitten to cheer me up, and we named her Tiffiny."

"That's interesting," Jamie said, thinking that the really interesting part was how fast she had told that story. She was talking so fast, he really had to concentrate to keep up with her.

"Do you have any pets?" Amanda asked.

"Do I have any pets?" Jamie repeated, feeling that she

was looking at him. Even though he wanted to look at her all the time, he just couldn't. He stared at the handlebars on his bike. "No. I don't have any pets."

"Not even a cat?" she asked. "Or a gerbil?" She giggled. "Oh, I think Mindy is coming out now! You have to go, so you won't know she's in the men's room! Pinky promise!" She held out her pinky and reached it to his. He quickly wrapped his pinky around hers, excited by the touch of her little finger against his.

"Pinky promise," he said, feeling ridiculous, but loving it anyway. He got on his bike and began to ride away.

"Remind me to tell you a funny gerbil story sometime!" she called after him.

He was looking forward to hearing her tell that story. What could be a funny gerbil story?

JAMIE
Now

"I wish I could have told you how I really felt about you. I wish I hadn't been bashful around other people so we could have stayed close friends. I haven't ever known anyone else like you. I haven't ever liked anyone else as much as I liked you. You are the only girl I ever really wanted.

"You know, do you remember that time I saw you at Franklin Park, over by the museum, when you were waiting for your friend to come out of the men's room? You promised to tell me a funny story about a hamster... no, not a hamster, a gerbil. You never did tell me that story, and I have been waiting a few years, more than ten years, more than twenty years, wow, way longer than that! We never really had another good conversation after that, because after that was when you were in that accident.

"You have to wake up and tell me that funny gerbil story. Come on, Amanda. I know you can hear me. Did your cat eat your gerbil, or something like that? Come on, wake up. If you wake up and tell me your funny gerbil story, I will tell you anything you want to know about me. I'll tell you everything. Please, just wake up."

Amanda seemed to be smiling, but she didn't wake up. Jamie sat beside her, watching her, for about two hours, until he finally had to leave to go get something to eat.

MANDY

My friend, Tami, has invited me over to her house. When I go inside with her, she tells me her mother isn't home from work yet, but that we can walk to the store and get some candy. I have the most intense feeling of déjà vu, as if we have done this exact thing before, and I don't really want to go through it again. It always ends with us walking through a cemetery.

Before we leave the house, she wants to show me her gerbils. They are in a cage. One is hiding in the corner under some sawdust, probably hoping we can't see him, and the other is running frantically on a little metal wheel, running and running but not getting anywhere. She opens the door to the cage and grabs the one that was hiding and holds it in her hand. I don't want to hold it. She puts that one on the couch, and then takes the other one out of the cage and holds it for a minute. She puts it on the couch beside the other one. They both look like they are in a panic. They run down the couch and under the radiator. Tami's house has one of those old-fashioned radiators like we have in our classrooms at school.

Tami reaches under the radiator – it is not turned on right now – and grabs one of the gerbils by its tail and pulls it out from under the radiator. She cuddles it in her hand, like it's a little kitten or something cute, but I think it looks like a little rat.

"Get the other one so we can put them back in the cage, and then we can go to the store," she says.

I don't want to touch that little rodent, but I don't want to say no to Tami. I don't want her to think I am scared of it, but I am. I reach under the radiator and the gerbil runs away, a couple of feet, still under the radiator. I feel sorry for it, since it must think it got away from me, the giant monster.

Tami sees that I haven't caught it yet.

"Just grab it by the tail and pull it out," she says. "Then you can pick it up."

I decide to do this. I reach down and pull it by the tail. The tail comes off in my hand! I panic and look back at Tami. She is putting the other gerbil into the cage. I toss the tail under the radiator and take a step away from it.

"I can't get it," I tell her, afraid, thinking I killed it when I pulled off the tail.

"I will get it," she says. She reaches down, under the radiator, and pulls out the other gerbil, the one that now looks very small without a tail. She doesn't notice the tail is missing and she cuddles it in her hand and gives it a kiss on the top of its head. She doesn't notice that where its tail was a moment ago, now there is just a little bloody cord. She puts it back in the cage with the other one. I grab my sweater so we can leave the house before she examines the gerbils any closer. I see the tail, all by itself, under the radiator, as we go out the door.

We cross the street and we have to walk through the cemetery to get to the store. I don't want to walk over the bodies of dead people, but we have no way of knowing exactly where they are. It doesn't seem to be bothering Tami. She is walking and talking, as if we were anywhere else in the world.

I feel we are being so disrespectful. I also feel a chill, moving through the air and moving through my body. I don't want to read the names on the headstones, and I don't know

150

why I am afraid to look at them; but I am very afraid. I am acting brave, as my stomach is turning, recalling the gerbil with the bloody cord instead of a full tail.

EARNEST
Now

"I'm here to see Mrs. Amanda Peoples?" Earnest said at the reception desk of the hospital. He didn't mean it to sound like a question, but he was so nervous, so far out of his comfort zone. He thought about Sister Peoples, doing everything with a smile, even things she probably didn't want to be doing, and that thought gave him courage.

"Are you family?" the receptionist asked, looking at her computer screen.

Oh, no, what if he had come all this way, suffered the torture of riding on all those dirty busses, just to be rejected? He had to see her!

"Yes," he said, "her church family." That seemed to satisfy the lady, because she didn't tell him to leave or that he couldn't see her.

"She is in room 304," she said. "Do you know how to get there?"

"No," he said, shaking his head.

"Go down this hall, take the elevator to the second floor, take a left, go to the end of that hall, it's a really long hall, and take the elevator to the third floor. Take a right when you get out of that elevator and you will see a directory of rooms on that floor. Have a nice day."

"Thank you very much," he said, thinking that she must not be aware that the day was over, and it was late evening now. He was standing in front of the elevator waiting when he realized he should have asked if she were still in a coma or if she had awakened. Well, he would find out when he got there, and either way, he would be able to see her.

His heart was pounding, and he was sweating up a storm when he arrived on the third floor. His head felt like it was burning up! He had to remember to breathe! He walked down the exact center of the hallway in an attempt to feel his balance, even distance on his left and right. He liked that the hall was so symmetrical and so very clean. He found a water fountain and took a drink, in an effort to both cool down and slow down. He was so excited, so afraid, so worried, so jumbled. He wanted to sit somewhere and let this panic time pass him by, but he didn't see any waiting rooms.

Earnest saw the sign that pointed in the direction toward room 304 and stopped to lean against the wall for a moment before taking these final steps to his destination. What if she had awakened? What would he say to her? What if she woke up while he was there, and he had to be the one to have to tell her that her family had been killed in the accident? What if someone else was in the room with her?

He began to think that this was not a good idea. He had planned out the whole thing, every leg of the journey, but he couldn't make himself go the final distance. The finish line was just a few yards away, but he could not do it. His feet refused to move in that direction.

He began to say a prayer, to ask God again for strength, when he saw another man come out of room 304, a handsome man he had never seen before. Oh, why was he worried? She probably had a hospital roommate, and the man was visiting the other person. Earnest forced his feet to go to the room. When he got there, he double-checked the room number and saw that the door was open.

He stepped inside the room, suddenly feeling all the

weight of his backpack. He hadn't eaten anything from it – no place that they stopped was clean enough – so it was incredibly heavy. He dropped it onto a chair, then he turned his eyes to the patient in the bed.

That was not Sister Peoples! He glanced over to the other bed and saw that it was empty. He looked back at the patient, letting his mind absorb her transformation; it was her. She looked so small, so shrunken, and her face was gaunt, with deep purple bruises on her forehead and on her chin. She seemed to be sinking into the bed. She had all kinds of tubes going into her, but she was breathing on her own. She looked as if she were sleeping.

He stepped closer to her. He wanted to talk to her, but he was afraid of disturbing her. He pulled one of the chairs close to the bed so he could sit near her and watch her without bothering her. He sat quietly for a few minutes.

"Hi, Sister Peoples," he finally whispered. "It's me, Earnest, or Brother Earnest, like you always call me." He looked closely at her face to see if she had any kind of reaction. He had so many things he wanted to tell her, but he wasn't sure if he wanted her to actually hear him say these things. Well, he had come all this way all by himself, to see her, pushing through his fears and anxieties. He had taken a step towards bravery. Now was the time to keep it going, to speak to her.

"We have really missed you at church," he said, having so many things in mind to say, and not knowing what he was saying. "Do you know how long you have been here?" He didn't expect her to answer, but he just had to talk. He kept his voice quiet so anyone else would not be able to hear him.

"I came up here on the bus," he continued. "Oh, did you know we are in Seattle? We are in a hospital in Seattle and you have been here for more than two weeks, ever since your car accident. Do you remember the accident? I read about it in the news report but I'm sure it was more terrible for you. I hope and pray that you don't have any memory of it.

"It is so strange to see you here, because you are always so active and so involved in everything, and now you are lying here, helpless. I felt so bad when I heard what happened, and I am so sorry for your loss. I wonder if you even know how much you lost in the accident? Have you been in the coma for all this time? I suppose you have. You probably don't even know about the funeral. I'm sorry to be the one to have to tell you that your husband and two sons were killed in the accident. They died at the scene of the accident. It was a miracle that you survived. I knew you were taken to the hospital, but I didn't even know that you were in a coma until Saturday, when Pastor Brown mentioned it at the funeral. I was expecting to see you there, at the funeral.

"Oh, the funeral was so beautiful. There must have been more than five hundred people there. The church was packed. It was overflowing. There wasn't enough room for everyone to sit down. We were there for about three hours. Pastor Brown gave a chance for everyone who wanted to say something about your husband and your family to get up and speak. The service was so wonderful. I wish I would have recorded it so you could listen to all the nice things everyone said about your family. The whole time, my eyes were watering, I felt so bad for you.

"Your husband really had a big influence on a lot of people, many more than I ever thought. You probably already know that, but I was really amazed to hear so many people, even young people, tell about how the Lord used your husband to change their lives by praying with them and helping them make decisions about the direction of their lives, and how he helped people get back on their feet when they were getting out of jail or out of the hospital or graduating from high school or college. And so many people told about how they were spiritually dead before they came to our church, and how Pastor Peoples helped to open their spiritual eyes. You would have been really proud of him. Oh, I know you are proud of him. I could always see how much you loved him and respected him, and how you were the perfect wife for him, helping him in so many ways so he could do his best for the ministry."

He decided not to say anything about her sons. It brought tears to his eyes to even think about those two little caskets, and he didn't want to get choked up here, not now, anyway. He already had somewhat of a lump in his throat. He needed to keep his composure. He felt that she could hear him, on some level, and he didn't want to make her cry on the inside.

"You and Pastor were there for me when my mother passed. I don't know what I would have done or how I could have gotten through it all. You guys helped me with everything. I couldn't do it. I was in a state of shock and my brother and sister were of no help at all. The arrangements and the service and everything, you guys walked me through it, really. You were holding my hands when I really needed it most.

"So, now I am here for you. I just hope I can be as much of a comfort to you as you guys were to me. I want to do whatever I can to help you. When you get well and go home, I can help you with your cooking and housework and yard work, or whatever you need me to do. You guys made me feel like part of your family, so I want to do the same for you. Whatever you need, I'll do it for you. I want you to know, I am here for you, right here, by your side."

He would have stayed right beside her all day and all night if the nurse hadn't come into the room and asked him to leave for a little while.

"I won't be gone long," he whispered to Sister Peoples. "I'll be close by if you need me."

EARNEST
Then

Earnest sat in his apartment at his home computer, unable to work, unable to move. The room was dark, the curtains drawn. He was a mess, wearing an old T-shirt, slumped in his chair. His hair was nappy, his teeth felt like they needed to be brushed, and he didn't care. He had no hunger, no thirst, no ambition, no direction. His life no longer had purpose.

He hadn't been to church in nearly three months. The joy, the peace and the hope that had been part of his personality had evaporated when he had faced reality and accepted the fact that the lady he loved was not the one God wanted him to love. He had stopped listening to her messages he had saved on his answering machine; he had even stopped listening to the edited versions he had created of her messages.

He was lovesick. Why would God put him in such a situation, to be completely in love with a woman he could never have? Was this just a test of his will, of his obedience, of his denial of himself? His heart was aching and he could not get her out of his mind. He didn't love her just because his mother had so vehemently insisted that he avoid white women; he had no control over his feelings for Sister Peoples, his attraction for her, his attachment to her.

He pictured her in his mind, knowing he could never see her again. He couldn't go back to church and long for another man's wife.

The doorbell rang. He wasn't expecting anybody; it must be his mother. He was glad he always kept the door locked – she would just barge in if the door were unlocked. Who else would come to his door besides somebody selling something? He didn't need to move out of his chair to tell the intruder to go away.

To his horror, the door slowly opened. Oh, no! He hadn't locked it when he had come in from taking out the trash, because his hands had become soiled and he didn't want to touch the knob until he had washed them; then he had forgotten to lock it once his hands were clean.

"Earnest!" a shrill voice called. "Are you home?" It couldn't possibly be Sister Linda Gentle, could it? He was frozen in his chair, as much with fear as with extreme anger, as she marched into the room. Just as he was about to protest and insist that she leave immediately, he blinked his eyes to clear his jumbled vision. Sister Peoples glided through the doorway just behind Sister Linda. His worst nightmare and his fantasy dream girl were both in his apartment? He couldn't possibly be awake and experiencing this; nobody ever came to his home.

"Are you all right?" Sister Peoples asked gently. "Your mother said you've been sick, and you haven't answered your phone or returned our calls."

"Yeah, Pastor Peoples wanted us to come and check on you," Sister Linda said, chomping on her gum. She was anything but gentle, and he couldn't think the name everyone at church called her. "You got any coffee?" she asked, going into the kitchen.

Earnest was still too stunned to say anything. He felt his face turning the darkest shade of red, thinking of how awful he looked. What kind of impression was he giving the woman he loved?

Sister Peoples took a step closer to him, but still keeping a respectable distance between them. Earnest could smell her perfume, that sweet scent of Tabu, and he could see true concern for him on her face. "Are you okay?" she asked.

He interpreted that to mean, 'you look terrible.' He wished she would look away from him, and not right into his eyes, into his soul. She was going to know he loved her if she looked any more closely: he couldn't hide it from her.

"I couldn't find any coffee," Sister Linda grumbled, coming back from the kitchen.

"I don't drink coffee," Earnest said, his voice returning suddenly and more gruffly than he expected. He wanted to leap out of the chair, push Sister Linda out the door, and keep Sister Peoples locked inside with him. He attempted to pull himself upright in his chair, despite his protesting arms and legs, which had become accustomed to lounging in one position for hours upon end.

"You're not contagious, are you?" Sister Linda asked, laughing at her attempt to make a joke. Is sin-sick contagious? Earnest wondered.

"No, I am feeling much better now, thank you," he said, directing his answer to Sister Peoples. He really couldn't stand looking at Sister Linda.

"You must have been really bad, if this is better," Sister Linda said, smacking her gum. Oh, she could be thankful that his mother wasn't here to hear that disgusting sound.

"I'm getting ready to go to Texas in two weeks," he said, surprised at the words that came out of his mouth. Texas? Where did that come from? "I'm going to get my technology degree," he lied, without being able to stop the words from coming out of his mouth. What was a technology degree, anyway? He hoped they didn't ask.

"You are moving to Texas to get a technology degree?" Sister Peoples asked. "Well, that's great, you'll be able to get a really good job then." Did he detect a hint of disappointment? She wanted him to stay here! Did she want him to stay?

"Excuse me for a minute," he said, suddenly motivated to get out of the chair. He escaped into his bedroom and looked in the mirror, faintly hearing Sister Peoples's voice say, "We can't stay long." He hurriedly teased his hair with his pick, adding a little moisturizer, until it looked presentable. He slipped on a clean, pressed, white shirt and buttoned it quickly, then pulled a black sweater over it. He hastily changed from his grey sweatpants to a pair of black dress pants and slid his feet into his black loafers. He was in and out of his room within two minutes.

"You didn't have to get all dressed up for us," Sister Linda said sassily.

Not for you at all, Earnest thought. "Oh, no, I'm just getting ready to go to a meeting," he easily lied. He had to get them out of his home; he had no room for fire and ice, one setting his illicit passion aflame and the other causing him to freeze in sin by hating that sickening, make-up plastered, man-addicted silly goose. He shuddered just thinking about her. His senses were heightened, so aware of every aspect of the one he loved, so filled with disgust for the one he hated.

"Oh, we didn't mean to interrupt anything," Sister Peoples said apologetically. "We just wanted to check on you because we hadn't heard from you in so long. We wanted to be sure you are okay. We'll be on our way now." She looked right into his eyes as she spoke, and Earnest made the fatal mistake of gazing into her beckoning pools of brown. He was drawn to her and was afraid he would never be able to look away from those captivating eyes. She stepped towards the door, and Earnest involuntarily stepped towards her. He had never been this close to her before, except in church, and he could feel her breathing.

"I have to go to the bathroom before we go," Sister Linda announced. Ordinarily, Earnest would not allow her to use his bathroom, but he was captivated by Sister Peoples, so he let Sister Linda go, without a word. His attention was focused on Sister Peoples, Amanda.

She was about to say something when he suddenly, against his will, closed the gap between them so he was standing directly in front of her. She was looking into his eyes, so kindly, so trusting, so vulnerable, so desirable. Another force had control of him as he gently placed one hand on her shoulder. With his other hand, he lifted her chin to his face, and he closed his eyes as their lips met; so softly, so lovingly, so perfectly. He was lost in time as he kissed her, as his tongue so delicately sought hers. The moment lasted a lifetime while they were together. After a moment short of eternity, he so slowly closed his lips, still pressing them softly but firmly on her sweet, tender lips and he ended the kiss. Through nearly-closed eyelids, he could see that her eyes were closed as she moved in slow motion, one millimeter at a time, away from him. His arms were around her as they realized what was happening to them, between them, his hands resting so gently on her. She was not going to vanish into thin air, like she always did in his dreams; she was really and truly here, alone with him, in the same place at the same time. He was filled with warmth and satisfaction; at the same time, excitement and anticipation. She stepped back one tiny step, two little steps. She had been here forever; she would be here with him forever; they were becoming one, together. She looked at him with an unusual look in her eyes; was she confused? Was she angry? Her eyes locked on his. What was the matter?

Oh, no; oh, no, no, no! What had he done? He had just

kissed his pastor's wife, and not with a holy kiss, but with a kiss that was most definitely unholy. He could still feel her soft lips on his – his lips that could no longer speak. He could not tell another lie with lips that had touched her lips. His lips were tingling! A warm sensation was pouring from the top of his head to the back of his head, down his neck, through his back, into his inner being. He slowly brought his hands away from her body, back to himself, creating a space between them; a space, but not an empty space.

Was she expecting him to say something? His hearing was filled with a loud noise. Her lips were moving – was she saying something? His heart was pounding – could she hear it? His sweater must be pulsating with each heartbeat. He was so close to her, he could feel her body heat, radiating, leaping the distance from her to him. His mind was racing around a racetrack, so fast, in circles, not stopping to make any sense. The two of them were worlds away from the drab apartment, standing together on a disk at the edge of the universe, at the end of time. They could take each other's hands and jump off the edge of reality into a world of their own. A ticking sound had become wedding bells, the air a blanket around them, the atmosphere charged with something more powerful than electricity.

What had he done? Had they really kissed, or had he imagined it? As he let his arms fall to his sides, he realized Sister Peoples had been hugging him, ever so slightly. Why wasn't she saying anything? She looked more beautiful than ever, now that she was a part of him, part of his real world, not just his fantasy.

"You need more toilet paper," Sister Linda announced loudly, her screeching voice cutting like a knife into Earnest's living dream. Sister Linda lumbered about, snooping around the apartment, oblivious to what was happening in the room. What was happening in the room? A thickness, a passion, a sweeping flood of emotion was raging and flowing and engulfing and encapsulating and... and... gone. The room was back to normal again, except with a shrill annoyance slicing through the otherwise wonderful moment. He felt an arrow piercing his back, between his shoulder blades, right to his heart. He hated Sister Linda.

"Well, glad to see you're still in the land of the living," Sister Linda said, opening the door, letting the extremely harsh sunlight into the room. Somehow Sister Peoples slipped away from his everlasting grip and she followed Sister Linda out the door, moving like lotion being poured out of a bottle, as she stepped out of his darkness, into the light.

Earnest didn't know how long he stood there, reliving the moment. Had it really happened? Had he really kissed the woman he so desperately loved? Had he really held her? Had they really been transported, together, to a place beyond comprehension?

It had not been a dream. He could still smell the Tabu. He put his hand to his face and inhaled her scent, still lingering on his palm. He had accomplished his goal; he had kissed her, and it had been wonderful. They had something special together, something between them.

He hated himself. She belonged to another man; she was not his. She could never be his. He was a terrible person. He had to get her out of his mind. He had crossed the line; he had betrayed his pastor. Why couldn't she have been any other woman in the world? Why did she have to be the pastor's wife? Because... she was the one he loved. She was the one who put a sparkle in his eye, a skip in his step, a leap in his heart. He didn't choose to love her!

How could she do this to him? He hated her! She shouldn't have kissed him! She shouldn't have come to his home! She shouldn't have invaded his privacy! She shouldn't have touched his heart and made him love her! She shouldn't have moved to this town and married the pastor! She shouldn't have such tender lips that pressed ever so softly against his!

He began to weep. He made his way to his chair, his chair that until today had been so safe, and crumbled into it. He had forced her to kiss him and she had liked it! She was so awful, so unfaithful, she could never be trusted! He could never look at her face again, could never again see those tender, loving brown eyes, those questioning eyes, or those lips that had been defiled against his lips.

How long had she been in his presence? Had hours or days passed, or just a moment? Each second had stretched into time immeasurable while they had taken their infinite journey together. She had been made for him – why had she married another man before Earnest met her?

His head dropped to his chest and he became aware that his nice black sweater was soaked with his tears. He was all dressed up. He had told her a lie... no, more than one lie. What had he said? That was the problem with lying. You had to remember what you said and to whom. He could never lie again. He made a resolution at that instant to always, from this moment forward, to tell the truth in every situation.

A knock on the door startled him. She was back! She was leaving her husband and coming back to him, to be with him forever! No, he wouldn't allow it. Their passion for each other had to end; it was the proper thing to do, the noble thing to do, the only thing to do. He wanted so desperately to welcome her into his home, his life. He forgave her for everything; he just wanted her to come back and stay with him. He needed her; his life meant nothing without her. They could move to another city, another state, and start a new life together. She now realized she had been made for him, and he was the one man who could truly make her happy. He had to let her in!

Before he could move, the door opened. For the second time in one extraordinary day, he hadn't locked it. Or was it still the same day? He held his breath in anticipation: he knew without a doubt, she had returned to him, alone, without Sister Linda, she was here to stay with him. He leaped out of his chair, ready to welcome her with open arms. His heart stopped beating.

"Earnest!" his mother's criticizing voice said, destroying his hopes for a future with Sister Peoples. "You know it isn't safe to leave your door unlocked."

"I know," he said, disappointed and suddenly exhausted. He collapsed into the chair.

"Why are you all dressed up?" she asked. "This place is a pig sty!" She eagle-eyed every item that was out of place. "Your good sweater is soaked! Do you have a fever? What are you doing in those clothes? Are you going somewhere? What's that I smell? Was somebody here? Do you have a woman here? Is a woman hiding in your bedroom? You are a good Christian man, and I know that you are well aware that is no way for a good Christian man to behave," she said, poking her head into the bedroom. "Oh, look at that bed! That is disgusting! Is she hiding in the bathroom? You come out of there, Sweetie, and face me like a woman! You can't hide from me!"

"Mom!" Earnest shouted, suddenly enraged. What if Sister Peoples had been in there? "You have no right to come in here like that! I am 45 years old! If I want to have a woman in here, that is my business, not yours!"

"You are part of me, and if you have a bad reputation, that reflects on me! Do I have to remind you that I am a pillar of this community, and Christians around here look up to me? If my son is sinning with a woman, you are likely to drive them away from the church and they will think our Christianity is just a sham! My love for Christ goes beyond just the talk! I live for Him and I expect you to do the same!"

"Mom, will you please go?" Earnest felt like pushing her out the door.

"Who are you hiding in there?" she demanded. "You are well aware—"

"It's Sister Peoples!" he shouted, against his will. That was not a lie; she *was* hiding in his heart.

His mother looked at him, shocked, stunned. She stood, unmoving, for the longest time, then she began to laugh. Was she going crazy, or was she having some sort of an episode? Maybe she was having a breakdown.

"I'm sorry," she said, giggling like a teenage girl. "I must have sounded crazy, going on like that. You get my point. I know you are a good boy. Sister Peoples! That's a good one. I was going a little overboard, wasn't I? You know where I'm coming from, don't you? I just want to protect you."

"Mom, you just want to protect your own reputation," Earnest said. "I would appreciate it if you would not come over here without calling first."

"Are you telling me I have to call you before I can come over to visit you? I have to make an appointment to see my own son?"

"That is what I am telling you," he said firmly.

"Well, for your information, my dear son, I have been trying to call you all day, and your answering machine is not working."

"I turned it off."

"You what? Are you telling me you turned off your

answering machine? What if it's an emergency?"

"Then, my dear mother, just call back until I answer," Earnest insisted, using an extreme amount of politeness. He had to get her out of here, before she recognized his guilt; or just in case Sister Peoples did decide to come back to him. He was the good boy in the family, and he couldn't let his mother have any idea that he had improper thoughts – or now, actions – toward and with Sister Peoples. "Now, if you will kindly excuse me, I need to go to an appointment, and I have to get ready."

"An appointment? Where are you going? I can give you a ride. You didn't tell me you had an appointment. You should have mentioned it to me. Here, I'll take you. You don't have to take the bus. I'll keep you company. It's a good thing I showed up, right when you need me. Why didn't you tell me you had an appointment today? I'll drive you. What kind of appointment is it, anyway? Are you all right? Are you feeling ill? Are you seeing some kind of specialist? Oh, it doesn't matter. You can tell me all about it in the car. I'll just wait until you get yourself ready."

With his mother's slow cadence of speech, it seemed to Earnest she would never finish making her point, for the second or third time. At this time, he was very tightly wound, emotionally, and he couldn't deal with being in the pressure cooker of his mother's voice or realm. Her very tone of voice was grinding down his spine.

"Goodbye, Mother."

"What?" she asked, too dense to understand what he meant. "What are you saying? What do you mean, 'goodbye, Mother?' Earnest, what are you saying to me?"

"It's time for you to leave, right now," he insisted.

"Don't you want me to drive you to your appointment?" she asked, unbelieving. "What if you need me afterwards?

What if–"

"Goodbye, Mother," he repeated, opening the door for her.

"You are forcing your mother to leave?" she asked angrily. "You are a good boy! You don't treat your mother this way!"

She lifted her nose into the air and left, as if it had been her idea to leave. Earnest closed the door behind her and locked it.

NICHOLAS
Now

Nicholas watched a nurse leave Mandy's room and he slipped in while she was again alone. He had to speak to her, to explain everything so she would understand how much he really loved her.

"I am so sorry, I let you get away from me," he said. He knew she was listening. She had a slight smile on her face. "When I came back in 6th grade, all the boys were teasing me. I thought you would know that my feelings for you hadn't changed. We promised each other. You made a promise to me."

He took her hand in his, noticing how cold it was. He softly rubbed it between his hands in an effort to warm it. She had to be feeling his touch.

"My biggest mistake, well, at that time, I'm sure you remember," he said, reliving that awful moment once again. "When the whole class was crowding around me when I came back from Montana in the sixth grade, and the guys said I loved you, I said, no, it was the other Nicholas that loved you, the new Nicholas. I saw the hurt in your face and I immediately wanted to take it back. I wanted to talk to you alone and explain it, but we didn't have a chance to be alone. Then you started to avoid me, and how was I to know that the new Nicholas really did like you? You began talking to him, and he started acting like he was your boyfriend. Then when he and his family moved away to Spokane, just about a month later, I wanted us to get back together, like we were before, but I didn't know how to do it. I didn't know what to say. Even when you came up to me and talked to me, I couldn't say it. I don't know why. I was a little bit mad, in a way, because I thought you should *know* how I felt, you should just feel what I felt. And really, I was mad at myself because I didn't make it right. I should have just told you how I felt, but how could I? Why didn't you know? I was so afraid that you didn't like me anymore, since I said that about the new Nicholas liking you. Then you seemed like you liked him, even more than you liked me, but I thought it was because you were mad at me.

"I didn't know what I could do to get you back after I hurt you like that. I was afraid you hated me, and not knowing if you did or not was better than finding out the truth, if the truth was that you did hate me."

He began to cry. Telling the truth did hurt.

NICHOLAS
Then

The 8th grade dance was held in the gym right after school on a Wednesday. Nick had overheard a week ago – no, he hadn't been eavesdropping, he just happened to be in hearing distance when Mandy and Mindy were talking about going to the dance – that Mandy was planning to go to the dance, but Mindy was planning to watch the cheerleaders practice instead. This bit of information made Nick so happy. He kept going over in his head what he was going to say, how he was going to approach Mandy, and how they would dance together, without Mindy interrupting them. They would not be able to dance every dance together, because the guys would never stop teasing him, but he would ask Mandy to dance, and they would have a chance to talk.

Many of the kids had dressed up for school that day, so unusual in junior high. Nick was so hot all day, with his dress shirt and sweater adding to his increased temperature of nervousness. He caught a glimpse of Mandy in the hall wearing her pretty blue dress, the most beautiful dress he had ever seen, looking so self-conscious. He wanted to be the one to make her feel comfortable, but he knew he had to wait until the dance. He had everything planned out: he'd tell her she looked pretty, ask her to dance, and while they were dancing, he would be able to tell her everything and convince her to go steady with him. By the end of the day, she would be his girl again, just like she was supposed to be.

He had to make sure he wasn't the first boy at the dance, so he hung around outside until he saw Kevin, Tony and Mark going into the gym and slipped in behind them. The room looked so different with the lights dimmed and all the streamers and balloon decorations. He waited a minute for his eyes to adjust to the darkness so he could look for Mandy. The bleachers had been stacked all the way back, so the gym looked enormous. The music, a fast song, was blasting, but nobody was dancing.

All the boys were lined up against one wall and all the girls were lined up against the opposite wall. Everybody seemed to be waiting for somebody else to go first, as they giggled and watched the ones across the room. Another song played and still, nobody danced. Nick spotted Mandy, but she was looking down at the floor, so she didn't see him. He tried to will her to look at him. As soon as she looked at him, he would go over and ask her to dance. She looked so pretty over there, she could have been the only girl in the room.

A slow song started, and Nick knew he had to wait until the next song. He couldn't be the first boy to walk across the vast expanse to the girls' side and ask Mandy to dance, not during a slow song. Mandy looked up, right at him, and he lost his nerve. He glanced around, suddenly particularly interested in a bunch of green and silver balloons. His face was on fire, his heart was pounding, and those balloons were just swishing back and forth. He knew they were yearning to break free from their tether and float up to the ceiling, just like he was yearning to break free from this line of boys and float over to Mandy. Somehow, the balloons were calming him, and he couldn't look away from them. They couldn't get away and neither could he.

When he finally was able to tear his eyes from the safety of the balloons, he saw that a few people were dancing to the slow dance. These were all established couples who had been going steady, and they were attracting the attention not only of the rest of the kids at the dance, but all the chaperones, who were making sure they weren't getting too close. He sneaked a peak at Mandy, who was talking to a girl next to her.

The two girls began walking slowly across the gym to the boys' side, making a huge arc around the dancing couples, and Nick felt his heart begin to pound even harder. She was coming to ask him to dance! Okay, he could deal with that. He hadn't been brave enough to go to her, but she was coming to him! Think of what you are going to say, he told himself.

All of a sudden, she was gone! Then he realized that she and the other girl had merely crossed the room to go to the rest room, which was on the boys' side of the gym. He decided to inch his way toward the rest room door so he could accidentally be right there when she came out; but he was too slow. She and the other girl came out quickly, just as the slow dance ended, and began to walk back across the room. To Nick's horror, he saw that the back of Mandy's dress was tucked into her stockings, revealing her legs and her bottom to the line of boys on this side of the gym!

The boys began nudging each other, and soon they were all laughing hysterically. Nick felt like crying, especially when Mandy arrived at the line of girls and one of them whispered something to her. She turned her back to the wall and pulled her dress down, with the help of another girl, and she burst into tears. She ran out the side door, leaving the dance. A chaperone shouted after her that she would not be able to re-enter, but that didn't stop Mandy.

"Did you see that?" Kevin asked Nick, poking him in the ribs. "She is such a dork."

Nick, his face red as a fire engine, had missed his chance

to talk to Mandy. Each day after that, she became harder and harder to approach; until finally, the school year ended, and his dad sent him back to Montana.

MANDY

I am all alone, wondering where everyone is. I am upstairs in my childhood bedroom, where I can hear the neighbors and their friends talking, their voices drifting up through my open window. They must be having a party in their driveway, with all those voices right under my window. I don't know why I should not be here alone, but I feel oddly left. I walk over to the window, to see the neighbors, although I don't want them to think I have been eavesdropping. I can't really understand them, the mumbling and rising and falling of voices. I just want to confirm that I am not alone.

I look out the window, standing back so I can't be seen, but no one is out there. The driveway is empty, and their door is closed. I can see in their windows. Nobody is home.

Yet I still hear the voices, coming in and going out, rising and falling. I try to understand what they are saying. The muffled conversation morphs into laughter, also rising and falling, like someone is messing with the volume.

Who is speaking? Why can I almost understand, but not quite?

What don't they want me to know?

JAMIE
Then

Jamie dug down to the back of his sock drawer, shoving the huge mass of mateless socks to the right and left until he found his special sock, the one with his wad of money hidden inside it. He pulled out the bills, glancing at his bedroom door to be sure it was closed. It was. He began to smooth the bills on the floor behind his bed. If his dad came in, he wouldn't be able to see all this money on the floor and wouldn't ask him what he was doing with so much money.

His heart was pounding in his chest – not because of the amount of money, but because of what he planned to do with it. He counted out two hundred dollars in tens and twenties, then added another twenty-five, just to be sure he had enough. He stuffed the remaining bills back into the sock without counting them. He had lots of money, it didn't matter how much he had. His dad gave him five dollars every day for lunch, completely disregarding the school newsletter that stated school lunch had been raised from 35 cents to 50 cents. Jamie accepted the money without argument, but he didn't want to take that much to school and attract any attention to himself. Every two weeks he bought a ticket for five dollars and he kept the rest safely tucked away in his sock.

After neatly folding the stack of bills and putting them in his pocket, he got on his bike and pedaled up the hill on 40th to Westpark. He dropped his bike on the sidewalk and looked in the window at Parry Jewelers. He saw necklaces, bracelets and watches. They didn't have any rings on display. He slipped into the store, startled by the bell above the door as it opened.

"Good afternoon, young man," an old jeweler said. Jamie noted the multitude of cracks in his face, like a shattered mirror, before turning his eyes toward the jewel case. "Maybe a nice bracelet or necklace for your mother? We have some on special this month."

"Ring," he mumbled softly.

"Pardon me?" the man asked kindly. "Can I help you find something?"

"I want to buy a ring," Jamie said, barely able to speak. His pounding heart was beating so loudly in his chest.

"If you are looking for a friendship ring for your girl-friend, you can go to Tuft's Drug store," the man suggested. "They are only about five or ten dollars. Our rings here are very expensive."

Jamie shook his head.

"Okay, I can show you what we have over here, in this case," the man said in a tender voice, extending his hand the way the models did on game shows when they were display-ing the prizes. Jamie moved over to that side of the store.

"Are you looking for a mother's ring?" the jeweler asked. "We have a nice selection here. What you do is, tell me what month you were born, and I will find out what is your birth-stone. We place your birthstone into one of these settings, whichever you like. We have white gold, yellow gold and rose gold, and some are combinations of different kinds of gold. Do you have brothers and sisters? We can add their birthstones, if you like, either now, or later. Of course, it will cost more to add them later."

Jamie again shook his head, examining the rings under

the glass. Most of them looked like they were made for old ladies to wear.

"These are engagement sets over here," the jeweler said, "but I don't think you are getting engaged yet, are you?" Jamie could feel him smiling, the smile seeming to radiate into Jamie's personal space.

Jamie saw it, the ring for Amanda. In a group of rings with various colors of stones sat a plain silver ring with some kind of carvings in the band. It was similar to a friendship ring, like the ones Jerry and his girlfriend had exchanged, but this one was shinier, more delicate. He pointed to it through the glass.

"Oh, you like the white gold collection?" the jeweler asked, pulling the tray of rings out of the case and placing it on the glass counter. "Which one do you like?"

Jamie pointed to the one he liked, tumbling the words "white gold" over in his mind. The ring looked just like silver, but white gold sounded so rich.

"This one is $199," the jeweler said. "See the intricate markings? It has been hand-created, a one-of-a-kind ring. An excellent selection, if you are in the market for something very special. Is it for your aunt? Maybe for your sister? What size do you need it? I can resize it for free, if you need."

Did rings come in different sizes? In his mind, Jamie pictured Amanda's hands, small and dainty. He looked at his own hand and he knew her ring finger was the size of his pinky finger. He held up his left pinky.

The jeweler removed the ring from its spot in the holder and placed it on Jamie's pinky finger.

"Well, that couldn't fit any better," he remarked, rotating, then sliding the ring from Jamie's finger. The jeweler pulled out a ring box, polished the ring with a cloth and put the ring into the slot without getting any fingerprints on it. "Two hundred nine dollars and forty-five cents," he said. "That's with tax."

Jamie counted two hundred dollars, then added a ten-dollar bill and set them on the counter. The jeweler put the ring box into a small bag and gave it to Jamie, who left the store without his change, before the man could even count the money. Jamie huddled against the brick building and pulled out the ring box so he could examine the ring. It really sparkled in the sunlight. Jamie slipped it onto his pinky and put the bag and the box in his pocket before jumping on his bike. When he gave the ring to Amanda tomorrow morning, he wanted to know he had worn it before she ever put it on her finger. Tomorrow morning, he was going to ask her to go steady with him. Starting tomorrow, Amanda was going to be his girl.

JAMIE
Now

Jamie saw a man leaving Amanda's room, and he quietly entered with the most incredible case of déjà vu. He was once again visiting her in a hospital room, but this time, he was alone with her. This time, he would be able to talk to her. She looked so beautiful lying in the bed, so vulnerable.

"Everything got messed up when you got hit by that car. I bought a ring for you. I had it with me. I was going to ask you to go steady. I had the ring in my pocket. But when I came riding down Chestnut that morning, I was a little late."

He looked closely at her face.

"Can you hear me? I think you can. I am finally telling you everything, so you will know.

"That was the most painful sight I have ever seen in my life, seeing you lying on the ground like that. I knew it was you, even without your hot pink coat. I was hoping it was someone else, but I saw your yellow Schwinn, all smashed up, and then I really knew it was you! You were there, lying in the middle of the street, with all those people around you, and your hair was all over the place. I felt sick to my stomach. You lifted up your head, just for a minute, but you didn't see me at the back of the crowd, behind your head.

"And you were talking, but not in your voice. You sounded like you had the voice of a little girl, talking to a girl in the crowd, and then you talked to the policeman. You told him your name and your address and your phone number.

Then you went back to sleep. Then the ambulance came, and they put you on the stretcher. I was so afraid you were going to die, especially when I saw all that blood on your face.

"I went to visit you in the hospital, but you were unconscious the first three times I came. Then I came again, but there were so many other people in your room, I, well, you know me. I couldn't go in your room with all those people there. I wanted to give you the ring, but I never got another chance.

"After you got out of the hospital, everything was different. Everyone at school was always talking to you because of your body cast. Your mom drove you to school every day, so we never got to ride bikes together again. You were different. You suddenly had lots of friends. Even though you and I were still friends, we never were close after that.

"I'm not blaming you. It was all my fault, I know that now. I was too afraid to get close to you when all those other kids were around you. For the rest of my life – until now – I have been waiting for you. I know we were meant to be together. I had to go through a lot to get to this point in my life, but here I am now, with you, and I know it was meant to be. I don't know what your life has been like since we were in school together, but now we are back together again. I will stay here by your side until you wake up and we can finally make our life together. This is the time I've been waiting for. Everything in my life led me right here, led us right here."

MANDY

I am riding my bike again. It is brand new, not smashed up like after my accident, and I am going so fast! I am barely pedaling, but I am going so fast! No cars are on this street, and I would like to slow down, so I turn onto a sidewalk, then start riding on the grass. I am still going faster than I have ever gone, and the friction of the grass is not slowing the bike!

I am afraid I will hit something and crash, a sprinkler head or a rock or a hole in the grass, because I am moving so fast, the ground is a blur and I can't see if any obstacles are in my way!

I notice that my tires are a few inches above the ground, so I relax. That's right, I won't snag on anything if my tires are not touching the ground. I feel the wind blowing my hair, flapping my clothes.

I am going so fast, as I pass houses, I hear snatches of conversations within them. I can almost make out what they are saying. I fly by Mindy's house, and I hear her mother mention my name. I want to stop and go visit Mindy, since I haven't seen her in so long, but the bike has a mind of its own. It is not stopping anywhere near here!

Why is Mindy's mother talking about me? Is she still mad that I had my ears pierced? She can't blame me for anything Mindy has done. She is making her own way in the world, as it should be, and we are traveling different paths.

I just wonder, why am I traveling this path so quickly? I am not even going downhill; I am on level ground. It seems like I hear someone say that I am on level ground, as I fly past the last house before the orchard.

Will I ever be able to stop and hear what people are talking about in all these conversations?

JAMIE
Then

"Jamie!" his dad yelled up the stairs. "I'm leaving now! Your lunch money is on the table!"

"Okay," Jamie said, probably not loud enough for his dad to hear him, knowing it didn't really matter if he heard him or not. Jamie couldn't decide what to wear. Most of his clothes were brown or tan, but he wanted to wear something special today, something that would impress Amanda. He knew she felt the same way about him that he did about her – she had to feel it. He could tell by the way she looked at him with the sparkle in her eyes, the smile in her eyes just for him, that he was special to her. He put on a brown shirt, then changed to a tan shirt, fumbling with the buttons. He had to get going! He wanted to be waiting at the corner of Chestnut and 40th when she came down the hill so he could get right behind her and follow her to school. She would lock their bikes with her lock and they would have a few minutes alone together, since Jerry was coming to school late today, after his orthodontist appointment. Jamie would take the ring from his pocket and say – what would he say? Last night he had it all planned, exactly what he was going to say, but now he couldn't remember anything! He couldn't just ask her to go steady. He couldn't ask her to be his girl. He couldn't just hand her the ring. He had to say the right words! He was shy in general, but around Amanda he was also flustered.

He didn't have time to think about it anymore right now.

He would have to pedal like crazy to catch up with Amanda. He ran out the door and grabbed his bicycle. Before he started going, he dropped his bike on the front lawn and ran back into the house. He forgot the ring! He tumbled up the steps to his room, grabbed the ring from his dresser, stuffed it in his pocket, flew back down the stairs and out the door. He got onto his bike and was flying down Chestnut as fast as he could go, not even slowing at the stop signs.

As he came over the hill at 28th Avenue, a brown car was approaching, coming toward him in the middle of the street. He glanced at the driver – a short old lady who could barely see over the dashboard – as he whisked past the car, just a foot or so from her door, avoiding the cars in the too-small parking lane. Some of those old ladies thought they owned the road, just driving any kind of way, all over the place, not staying in their lanes. Jamie began to go faster, now that he was on the downhill stretch leading up to 40th, and was really speeding when he noticed a crowd standing in the street ahead of him.

As he got closer to 40th, he could see that the crowd had gathered in the middle of the intersection, with several cars on either side, blocking traffic. Someone must have had an accident; too many people for a dog to have been hit. There were at least 25 people standing, but he didn't see any damaged cars anywhere.

He put on his brakes and skidded to a stop just outside the crowd. As he looked to his left, time slowed as he felt himself going into a surreal, dreamlike state. A yellow Schwinn was crunched up just outside the crowd. Voices were low and distorted, as people moved in slow motion – or were they even moving at all?

No, this could not be happening. As one girl stepped out of the circle, Jamie could see another girl lying on the ground, face down. She was not wearing her bright pink coat, but he knew that brown hair, those curls, that were flying all over her head, touching the asphalt. No, no, she couldn't be dead. The thud of his heart told him it was Amanda. Why did it have to be Amanda? Why couldn't someone else be in an accident? Why did it have to be her?

Voices began to drift to his ears, which were filled with a roaring sound, and he tried to make sense of what they were saying.

"The car didn't even stop."

"She flew up in the air at least 20 feet!"

"Is she breathing?"

"Did you see her bike? It's all mangled."

"We were in the car right behind her. We saw it happen."

"Do you know who it is?"

"She's our neighbor."

"It was a hit-and-run!"

"I memorized the license plate."

"Did anyone call the police?"

"My brother is calling her mother right now. She lives next door to us."

"An ambulance is on the way."

"Don't try to move her."

"She's lifting up her head!"

Jamie felt himself swaying, sick to his stomach. He dropped his bike in the street and fell to his knees. When he looked again in the direction of the crowd, he could see her better now, between the legs of the onlookers. He still couldn't see her face – just as she lifted it a few inches, it fell, as if onto a pillow. It was on the ground. Her beautiful face was smashing into the street!

"I saw it happen," a boy confided in Jamie, speaking quickly. "I was walking on the sidewalk, right over there, and this car came up to the intersection. It stopped at the stop sign, then it pulled out a little ways, then it stopped again, then it pulled out a little ways more, then it stopped again, then it started to go. Then it stopped right in the middle of the intersection, and the bike came flying down the hill. She couldn't stop, she was going so fast! And the car stopped right in front of her, and the bike plowed into the car and she went flying up in the air, about 20 feet! Then she came down and bumped her head on the car, then the car drove away, and she hit the ground. I don't think the driver ever even saw her! I saw the whole thing!"

The sound of a siren pierced Jamie's ears. Suddenly several police officers were there, pushing their way through the crowd, asking people to step back.

"Does anyone know the identity of the girl?" one officer asked, as another put his fingers to her neck to take her pulse.

"She's alive," the second officer said.

Jamie let out a breath he didn't realize he was holding.

"She lives next door to us," one high school girl said. "Her name is Mandy, Amanda. We were right behind her in our car and she was on her bike. A car just pulled out in front of her, from Chestnut, right there, and she was going down the hill so fast, and the car stopped right in front of her. She couldn't stop. Her bike hit the car and the car just drove away. My brother went to that house over there to call her mother."

"I saw it!" a little boy shouted. "She flew up in the air! And then she came down on the car and the car drove away and she landed on the street."

"Did anyone get the license plate of the car?" one of the

officers asked.

"I wrote it down!" a girl said, handing the officer a piece of paper.

"It was a brown car," Amanda's said, sounding like a little girl, not moving from her uncomfortable spot on the street.

The crowd was silenced as all eyes turned to the girl lying in the middle of the street.

"It WAS a brown car," a boy confirmed, nodding his head frantically.

Jamie thought about the brown car that had passed him just a few minutes ago – or was that a few hours ago?

"Can you tell me your name?" one of the officers asked, as he squatted down beside Amanda.

"Mandy," she said in that little girl voice. "Mandy Foster."

"Where do you live, Mandy?"

"North 48th," she answered, still not moving her head.

"Is she awake?" someone asked. "Her eyes are closed."

"It's like she's talking in her sleep."

Jamie was feeling dizzy, unable to tear his gaze away from the most terrifying sight he had ever seen in his life.

"Here comes the ambulance," a boy said, jumping up and down. The crowd parted to let the ambulance move in close to Amanda. Jamie was frozen in place as a team of men moved in with a stretcher. He watched them as they checked her, feeling for broken bones and gently lifted her, turning her onto her back. Jamie gasped when he saw her face, covered with blood. Her mouth was closed, but he could see her teeth through a hole in her chin. He stared at her blood on the pavement, his eyes fixed on that spot.

They whisked her away in the ambulance, siren blaring, as Jamie pulled his thoughts together. He had to go to the hospital. He scrambled for his bike as the crowd was dispersing, people going about their day and reviewing the details of the accident. Jamie turned around and went back up Chestnut, a shortcut by bike to the hospital. The ambulance had gone down 40th to Tieton Drive, but Jamie's fastest route would be to go on Chestnut.

His head was pounding as he approached the back side of the hospital, such a familiar sight. He had spent many evenings here while his dad was working. He had mastered the art of being the invisible boy, able to slip through the corridors of the hospital where kids under the age of 14 were forbidden to go, all hours of the evening and through nights when his dad was doing emergency surgery. He knew the ambulance would take Amanda to the emergency room, and he knew how to get there without being seen.

Jamie walked in a calm manner, not betraying his anxiety, toward the emergency room. Nurses and orderlies passed him without notice, without asking why he wasn't in school, without wondering why he was in this part of the hospital by himself. He recognized some of them – they worked with his dad – but he was invisible to them.

"Jamie!" his dad's surprised voice said in a half-whisper, half-shout. "What are you doing here?"

"My friend just got hit by a car," Jamie said, his voice trembling. "I need to see–" he stopped before saying 'her' and quickly changed his sentence. "Can I go into the emergency room?"

"Didn't you comb your hair this morning?" his dad asked, trying to comb through Jamie's little mop with his fingers. "Or brush your teeth? Jamie, don't you look in the mirror before you leave the house?"

"I rode my bike," Jamie said, not wanting to waste a precious moment.

"You have a bus pass," his dad said. "You don't need to ride your bike all the way to school."

"Yes, I do," Jamie protested, looking anxiously down the hallway.

"Let's go check on your little friend," his dad said, putting his hand on Jamie's shoulder, to lead him to the emergency room waiting area.

"No, Dad, that's okay," Jamie said. "I can go by myself."

"You shouldn't even be here by yourself," his dad said, in his lecture voice, still steering Jamie by his shoulder. "You shouldn't be here, period. It's a school day."

Jamie resigned, wondering how he was going to tell his dad that he was here to see a girl, one who was almost his girlfriend. He just remembered the ring! He reached into his pocket – it was still there. A scene flashed through his mind: he would be standing next to her hospital bed, alone in the room with her, and he would give her the ring. She would tell him that she would love to be his girlfriend, and he would put the ring on her finger, and she would give him that smile, the sparkly-eye smile she had just for him, and they would hold hands as he gazed into those eyes.

"Jamie! Are you listening to me?" his dad asked.

"Mm-hmm," Jamie said, so rudely brought back to reality by his dad's insistent questioning. They were standing in the hallway that lead into the emergency room area, one door leading to the waiting area, the other door for the doctors, going into the emergency room.

"What is your friend's name?" his dad asked, his tone giving Jamie the impression that he had already asked him that same question.

Jamie looked at the floor, noting a small candy wrapper near the wall on the otherwise spotless waxed hallway.

"Dr. Sanderson?" a nurse said, as she rushed into the hallway. "We need you right away," she said, pulling him into the doctors' emergency door.

Jamie slipped in behind them unnoticed.

"Emergency stitches," he heard her say, as she whisked his dad behind one of the curtains. Jamie glanced to the left and right and saw that there was only one occupied bed in the emergency room. It had to be Amanda. He stepped behind the curtain, behind his dad and the nurse and saw her lying on the bed. Her face was still covered with blood, but now it was dried, as the nurse was dabbing the area surrounding the cut on her chin. His dad was washing his hands.

Amanda's eyes were closed, but she was talking.

"Is it Jamie's dad?" she asked. Her question was ignored. "Is Dr. Sanderson Jamie's dad?" she asked. Her hand reached for someone, but no one was there.

"It hurts," she cried softly. "Where's my mom?"

"Shhh," the nurse said, giving her a shot in the chin.

Jamie felt a tear slide down his cheek. He hadn't cried in years! But this was for Amanda's pain. He wanted to step out of his hiding place and hold her hand – but he didn't. He watched – as he had so many times before – his dad at work, as he stitched Amanda's chin. Jamie looked at her closed eyes. They fluttered open! She looked around, her eyes not focusing, but zeroing in on him. She seemed to be staring at him, trying to recognize him! Her eyes slowly closed.

Jamie heard snippets of conversation in the room.

"Possible concussion."

"That should do it for now."

"Broken bones in left arm."

"I just gave her 20 cc's."

"Where is Amanda Foster?" a woman asked, with a cry being stifled. "She's my daughter! Is she going to be all right?"

Amanda's mother was brought into the room and she moved into position to block Jamie's view of Amanda's face.

"Mommy?" Amanda asked, again in that little-girl voice.

"I'm here, Sweetheart," her mother said, unable to hide the cry in her voice.

"I'm okay, Mommy," Amanda said, starting to cry as well.

"Yes, you are," her mom reassured her.

"Why are you crying?" Amanda asked.

"Because you are crying."

"I'm crying because you are crying."

"Let's don't cry," her mother suggested. She pulled herself together and stopped crying.

"Did you call Daddy?" Amanda asked, no longer crying, but still using her little-girl voice.

"Yes, I called him, and he is on his way," her mother said.

"I'm tired," Amanda said. "What happened?"

"Everything is okay now," her mother said, lightly patting her head, smoothing her matted hair.

When Amanda didn't answer, Jamie assumed she had fallen asleep. His dad began to speak softly to her mother, and Jamie slipped out of the room. He considered going to the waiting room, but what would he do there? That might invite a conversation with his dad, and he didn't want that right now. No, if he just went to school, by tonight his dad would forget all about this morning and they wouldn't have to talk about it. Jamie could come back and visit Amanda after school. She was all right and she would probably have to stay in the hospital for a day or two. Soon they would be riding bikes together again, but they would be closer. He was going to give her the ring and she would be his girlfriend.

JAMIE
Now

A man stuck his head in Amanda's room and Jamie's growing courage drained from him. He quickly scooted the chair away from the bed and slipped out of the room before he could be forced to talk to anybody about her.

He did love Amanda, but was he ready to announce it to the world yet? Short answer: no.

NICHOLAS
Then

"Grandma, you should get someone to help you with the housework," Nick said, as he dusted the end table.

"I can take care of it, Son," his grandma said. "I don't need someone else to come in our home. I was going to do the dusting today, but you beat me to it."

"Okay, Grandma, but if you need any help, just let me know. I'll pay for it," he said, finishing the task.

"Oh, Dear, you don't need to do that," she said. "I appreciate your offer, but you have medical school ahead of you and you will need all the money you have."

"Grandma, I have a full scholarship. Everything is paid for." He put up the duster and looked around the tiny living room, which had not changed since he lived here during grade school. The same dark green curtains flanked the tall, thin windows, the same light green carpet covered the floor, and the same grandma-type flowered sofa and matching chair were in the same place they had always been.

"I am so proud of you," his grandma said sweetly. "Boston is so far away, but you are living your dream."

Not completely, he thought. Yes, he had always dreamed of going to medical school, so he could be a doctor who would be able to help children, but in the back of his mind, he had thought Mandy would be with him. He didn't even know which college she had attended or where she lived now.

"You should call her mother," his grandma suggested.

"What?" he asked, a little flustered that Grandma always knew when he was thinking about Mandy.

"You are just here for Christmas, and she would like to hear from you. You can ask her where she lives now, just to be friendly and make conversation."

Conversation had never been his strong point, and phone calls were not his favorite way to communicate, but Grandma did have a point. He could just casually call Mandy's mother and ask about Mandy. He was going to do it right now, while he had the nerve, before he got too busy with Christmas errands, or whatever else his grandmother needed him to do.

He went to the kitchen to make the call. He didn't have to look up the number – he still knew it from when he had memorized it ten years ago.

The phone rang two times.

"Hello?" a voice answered. It didn't really sound like Mandy's mother's voice.

"Hi, good evening, is this Mrs. Foster?" he asked tentatively. This was one reason he didn't like making phone calls. He couldn't see who was speaking.

"No, this is Mandy," was the reply. "Can I tell her who's calling?"

Nick's voice stuck in his throat. She was home for Christmas also? Or had she moved back home after college? His Mandy was on the other end of the line?

"Hello?" she asked. "Are you still there?"

"Mandy," he said, the name precious in his mouth.

"Nick?" she asked. "Is this Nick?"

"Yes, yes, how are you doing?" His heart was beating just about out of his chest.

"Fine, great, well, how do you like all this snow?"

"This is a little bit, compared to what we have in Boston."

"Boston? You live in Boston?"

"I'm going to–" he stopped himself. He wanted to tell her in person. He wanted to see her again! "What are you doing tonight?"

"Tonight? Oh, we were going to make Christmas cookies, but we decided to do it tomorrow instead, so tonight, I'm not doing anything."

"Do you want to go out?" This was the question he had been wanting to ask her for so many years, but this was his first opportunity.

"Tonight?" she repeated. "Yeah, sure, that will be fun."

Fun wasn't exactly the word he would use to describe what he wanted the evening to become, but it was a start.

"I'll pick you up... oh, this is embarrassing," he admitted, not having thought this all the way through. This was what he got for acting on impulse. "I don't have a car here."

"We can go in my car, if you don't mind riding in a tiny Honda," she suggested. Was that eagerness he detected in her voice?

"Then it's up to you," he said. "What time do you want to pick me up?"

"How about 6:30," she said. "Is that too early? Will you be finished with dinner by then? Or is that too late?"

"No, 6:30 is perfect," he said. He wanted to add 'and so are you,' but he held his tongue on that one. He began to sweat. He hadn't dated anyone all during college, because the only girl in his heart had always been Mandy.

"Okay, I'll see you at 6:30," she said. "At your grand-mother's house, right?"

"Yes, that's where I'm staying," he said.

"Oh, before I hang up," she said, making his heart skip a beat with anticipation, "did you want to talk to my mom? You asked for her when you called."

"Oh, no," he said with a chuckle. "I was calling to ask her about you. I didn't know you would be there."

"Then it all worked out," she said. He could imagine her smile as she said it.

"Yes," he said, thinking that it hadn't all worked out yet, but he was hoping it would tonight.

"Okay, see you at 6:30," she said, adding, "don't worry, my car might be small, but it has a good heater."

"Great," he said, thinking that heat was the least of his worries, even though the temperature was only in the 20s. He was so hot right now, he felt like taking off his shoes and shirt, something he would never do at his grandmother's house.

"Bye," she said.

"Bye," he answered, waiting to hang up the phone until he heard it click.

"Did you talk to her mother?" his grandmother asked, coming into the kitchen.

"Mandy was there, and she answered the phone and I talked to her," he said, feeling off balance and light-headed.

"That is so wonderful," his grandmother said with a sparkle in her eye.

"We are going to go out tonight, together," he said, feeling like he was stumbling over his words. Why should he be nervous around his grandmother? He was just going out on a date – was this really going to be a date? – with an old friend, one of his oldest friends. No, he couldn't kid himself. She was the girl he loved, the girl he wanted to make his life with, the only girl he dreamed about.

He wondered what she looked like now. Did she have long hair, like the last time he saw her? He hadn't seen her since they were in the 8th grade, when he never did work up the courage to talk to her again. He had spent many hours talking to the school counselor about her, but he had let her slip away from him, without telling her how he felt about her.

He looked at the clock. It was only 2:30 now. Did he have enough time to get ready? He had to take another shower – he was covered with sweat now, and he would have to eat dinner before she came, since Grandma had dinner ready at 5:00 every evening.

How could he eat? Was time passing too slowly or too quickly? He had gone all through college following every rule, passing every class at the top of the class, but now he could not think of what to do! Mandy had him all rattled again, and all they had done was speak on the phone! He loved her so much, he had always loved her, and tonight he was going to tell her!

NICHOLAS
Now

"I blamed you for so long for everything," he said to her sleeping self. "I couldn't believe that you loved someone else. I thought you betrayed me."

He knew she could hear him; she had to hear him, so she would know how much she had always meant to him. He moved closer to the hospital bed.

"I tried to move on. I met someone, a girl, who did not look at all like you, because I didn't want to be reminded of you. But I couldn't help comparing her to you. She was pretty, but not as pretty as you. She was smart – she's a lawyer – but she wasn't as smart as you. She was nice, but she never looked at me the way you did. She just never did love me the way I knew you would love me.

"I blamed you because I didn't want to blame myself," he confessed. "I should have answered that last letter you sent me. If I had answered, would you have come to me? I read it about a hundred times. I was still hurting because you told me you had another boyfriend, but when you told me he left you, I couldn't answer. I wanted to be your first choice, not your back-up plan. It was my fault, even before that. I should have spoken up when we went out. I should have told you how I felt about you. I should never have let you go that last time."

MANDY

I am working at a TV station, and I love it! I feel so blessed to have such a great job. I am sitting in the control room where 30 monitors are on the wall in front of me. Different action is happening on every monitor, but only one has the audio on, the on-air monitor. That is the one that requires all my attention.

I glance around at the monitors and see news feeds from around the world, ancient sit-coms, weather notices, and snippets of sports stories. All those things have relevance to the members of the news team, but my focus must be fixed on the video quality of the on-air monitor. The feed is coming by microwave from New York City. We have a parallel feed by satellite that is delayed by the one second it takes to beam from New York to the satellite and back to us. That video is a bit snowy, but it will do if we lose the microwave feed. The worst thing we can do is let the station go to black. I am prepared to immediately switch to satellite if necessary.

The audio from the on-air monitor is a bit jumbled. I can't understand what the actors are saying. I know they are speaking English, but it is fading out and getting muffled. We have all these video options, but only one audio stream, unless I switch to the satellite, which has its own audio, which I am unable to preview. This system does not allow splitting of audio and video, so what should I do? The rule is, don't change to satellite unless we lose microwave, or if we lose the audio.

I switch to satellite, see the one-second delay, which viewers at home just see as a little glitch, and I realize the audio is messed up on this feed, too! I quickly switch back to microwave. Better to have excellent video than to have both video and audio problems.

I become aware that I am the only person in the whole TV station. Where are my co-workers? Where has the engineer gone? Who can help me fix this audio, so the words can be understood?

Why is the pressure, the responsibility of this whole broadcasting system, all on me?

NICHOLAS
Then

Nick changed his shirt three times before he decided to wear his dark blue sweater over his light blue dress shirt. He had put on four different ties before he realized that he looked too dressed up for tonight's meeting with Mandy. This was going to be a casual evening; and besides, here on the West Coast, the people didn't dress as formally as they did on the East Coast. Even the newscasters on TV out here seemed to be more relaxed, as if they were trying to be familiar with their audience.

"Nick, your little friend is here," his grandmother called.

She was a few minutes early! He liked that. He hadn't heard the doorbell. Maybe she had knocked, or maybe his grandmother had opened the door when she saw Mandy approaching.

He took one last look in the mirror, nervous that he was forgetting something. He wanted to give her a gift, perhaps jewelry, but he had hadn't had time to go shopping. He hadn't expected her to be here, but now she was HERE, right here, at his grandmother's house.

He walked into the tiny living room and saw Mandy giving a Christmas card to his grandmother. They didn't notice him at first, and he stood there, observing their conversation for a moment. Mandy's beauty took his breath away. She looked the same as she had ten years ago, only more beautiful, more mature. She was being so gracious to his grandmother, smiling, talking. He didn't tune in to what they were saying, he just watched the scene until he realized this was happening now, and he needed to be a part of this, she needed to be back in his life, starting right this minute.

"Hi," he said, trying to force himself to overcome his shyness around her.

"Hi, Nick!" she exclaimed. Her face lit up when she saw him – he saw a light go on inside of her.

"Grandma, I'll be home later," Nick said, suddenly needing to get out of the house, to be alone with Mandy. "I have my key, so you don't need to wait up." He knew she often went to bed by 8:00.

"You two have a wonderful time together," his grandmother said, with a smile that said she knew what a special evening this was going to be for them.

"Where do you want to go?" Mandy asked, as they got into the car.

"I don't know, anywhere you want to go," he said. "I don't really know any places around here."

"We could go to Red Robin," she suggested, "but it's really noisy in there. No, let's not go there."

"Let's go somewhere that's not so loud," he said.

"Are you warm enough?" she asked. "It takes a few minutes for the heater to warm up."

He was burning up, but he couldn't tell her that. "I'm fine," he said. He looked straight ahead, not daring to look at her.

"I know!" she said suddenly. "We can go to the Bushwacker! Have you ever been there? That's where everyone our age goes, really. Remember Martin DeMinto? He played baseball for Wilson, then for Ike, then for the Beetles? Oh, that's right, you were gone then. Anyway, he owns it, and it's really nice."

"That sounds fine," he said, thinking that she seemed to be a little nervous.

"It's right downtown," she said. "I've only been there a couple of times, but it's really nice."

"Okay," he said, wanting to start a real conversation, but not knowing how or where to start.

"How long are you here for?" she asked, paying close attention to the darkened streets as she drove.

"I'm here until the day after Christmas," he said.

"Then where are you going?" she asked.

"Back to Boston," he said.

"You live in Boston? How do you like it?" She turned the little car onto Yakima Avenue.

"Oh, it's fine," he said, wondering how she would like to live there. "It's just a little more formal there than it is here."

"Really?" she asked. "That must be weird."

"It's not weird," he said, "just a little different."

"Okay," she said. "But isn't different kind of the same as weird?"

He forced a laugh. He wanted to be more comfortable around her, but he felt as if he were at a job interview and he had to say all the right things or he would be rejected. He had forgotten that she had a sense of humor. He didn't know how he could lighten up and not be so serious around her. He wanted her to have fun with him!

She parked her little car in a tiny parking space. They stepped out of the car.

"You know, if everyone in this country drove a Honda, we would have twice as many parking spaces," she said.

"Yeah, and twice as much room on the roads," he added.

"Exactly!" she said. "What kind of car do you have?" She pointed to the door of the restaurant. She took a step and slipped on a patch of ice on the sidewalk. He quickly grabbed her arm so she wouldn't fall.

"Thank you!" she said.

"Be careful," he said, as much to himself as to her. "I don't have a car," he said. "I don't really need one."

"Oh, that's cool," she said.

He didn't really like that phrase, but it was so popular these days.

They entered the slightly darkened establishment and were led to a table for two. Nick had hoped they could sit in a booth, but the place was nearly full and there were no empty booths. Mandy looked around the room, as if looking for someone.

"Oh! There's Tom Brewster and Mark Hammer!" she exclaimed. "Remember them? They were both in first grade with us, and we went all through school together! Do you want to go and say hi to them?"

"No, not really," he said. "I'd rather just sit here with you," he said, looking at her, wanting to take her hands in his. This was not the time to hold her hands, though, not yet.

She removed her coat and he saw how thin she had become. He hoped she hadn't been sick. She wore a dark red jacket with a pink blouse and black pants. She wasn't wearing any jewelry – not earrings, not a necklace, not even a ring. All the girls back East were always decked out in jewelry. However, Mandy did not look at all plain. Her makeup was minimal, but she was so beautiful and elegant just how she was. She was clearly the most beautiful girl he had ever seen.

"So, do you live here now?" he asked. They had so much catching up to do. He didn't know anything about her life since junior high school.

"Yeah, I've been back for about six months, since I graduated from college," she said.

"Where did you go to college?"

"I went one year to YVC, here, then I moved to Olympia to finish college and got my BA."

"In what?"

"Liberal Arts," she said, surprising him. She had always been so good with math, he thought she might have gone into engineering or perhaps become a stockbroker. "I did an internship at the TV station here, doing TV production, but I haven't been able to get a job in TV. I might go into advertising, if I can get into it. At first, I went into art, but then I couldn't really draw or paint, so I tried photography. That was really fun, then I discovered TV production, instant moving color pictures with sound, and I loved it. But the job market is really limited. I sent out 26 resumes and had three interviews, but, so far, I haven't been able to get a job."

Her interests had changed, but she still had the same mannerisms: tossing her hair that way, touching her face, wiping her jacket, almost unable to sit still.

"It was funny, I couldn't wait to move out when I was 18, but then, when I graduated from college, I really wanted to move back home," she said. "I just can't really find the place where I am supposed to be. I mean, there's not a job for me here in this small town, but there's not a home for me anywhere else."

This was his opportunity, the open door for an invitation to move back East – but no, it wasn't the right time. He had to go through medical school before they could get married, and they couldn't live together until they were married. Oh, sure, other people were doing it, but he had his standards and he knew she did, too.

IIe suddenly wondered if she had kissed any other boys besides him and he felt a pang of jealousy. She must have, either at her prom or some other time. He hadn't seen her in nearly ten years, and although he had not kissed another girl, he couldn't expect the same from her. But they had made a pledge to each other.

EARNEST
Now

Earnest saw the nurse walk by the family waiting room, so he knew he could go back to talk to Sister Peoples again. As soon as he entered her room, he noticed that her left hand was outside the covers. He reached down to cover it with the blanket. When he moved the blanket, his hand brushed against hers.

"Oh, Sister Peoples, your hand is so cold." He held her hand between his hands to warm it, and he noticed that her skin felt dry.

"Isn't anyone taking care of you?" he asked. He reached into his backpack and found his bottle of natural skin lotion. He put a dab into his hand and rubbed his hands together, to warm the lotion. When it was warm, he gently rubbed it into her hand, lovingly using both of his hands.

As he was doing this, a nurse came into the room. He was startled and pulled his hands away from her hand.

"Oh, don't mind me," she said, "I just have to write down her numbers." She grabbed the clipboard and walked over to the bank of monitors on the other side of the bed.

Earnest didn't know what to say, so he just continued what he was doing, rubbing the lotion tenderly into Sister Peoples's hand.

"Here, I can give you her other hand," the nurse said, pulling the right hand from beneath the blanket and setting it on her stomach.

"Her hands are so cold," he said, as he began applying lotion to her right hand.

"That sometimes happens when people don't move around for a few days," she said. "She hasn't complained."

"Can't you do something about it?" he asked, while stroking and warming this cold hand with both of his. "For her?"

The nurse looked up from the clipboard and smiled at him. "You love her, too, don't you?"

He was shocked at this statement, this declaration. He *did* love her, but nobody else knew that.

"I'll tell you what I'll do," she said, leaning over Sister Peoples, as if conspiring with him. She looked to the left and right, making sure no one else was listening to what she was about to say. "I can bring a her a warmed blanket. I'm not supposed to bring one to a patient unless they ask, but no one will be the wiser. You won't tell anyone, will you?"

"No," he answered, shaking his head. "I really thank you for that. She needs to be warm."

"Well, Honey, there's no rule that says you can't climb in bed with her and warm her up with your body heat," she teased.

She noticed the seriousness on his face and quickly changed her expression. "I'm just kidding, of course we have a rule against that. I'll be right back with the warmed blanket."

EARNEST
Then

In an unexpected way, Earnest's life took an interesting turn when his mother had a stroke. His mother had been so health-conscious; or she had appeared to be as such, that the news of her having a stroke was a huge surprise. His brother, Robert, and sister, Carolyn, came to town to visit her when she was in the hospital. Carolyn took Earnest with her the one time she visited her. Earnest was so shocked to see their mother lying there, helpless, unable to speak. Carolyn took advantage of the moment, to tell her mother she loved her in one breath and to blame her for all the problems in her own life in the next. When his sister stepped out of the smelly hospital room, Earnest, exasperated, moved closer to his mother, who eyed him suspiciously, undoubtedly expecting him to be her next accuser. However, Earnest could not do that. Regardless of how she had treated him all his life, she was his mother, the one who had given him life, and his heart went out to her.

"Hi, Mom," he began, looking at her worried eyes for a second before casting his gaze out the window, a safer scene to be viewing for an encounter like this. "How are you feeling? Just forget about what Carolyn was saying. She's really upset and it's hard for her to see you like this. She really does love you. We all do. You had a very difficult job, raising us after Dad died, and we understand your struggle."

He glanced down to see his mother looking at him in a way she never had before: with hope and trust in him. At that moment, he knew he would be the one to take care of her, whatever it took. Her left side was paralyzed, and she couldn't talk, so it would be awhile before she would be able to take care of herself. She needed him.

"Don't you worry about anything, Mom," he said with a new boldness. "I'm going to take care of everything. I'm going to take care of you."

He knew he would have to power through any potential panic attacks to be able to get her affairs in order. He didn't really have any idea of what was going to be involved with this process, but he did know one person who could help him, one person who had the skills and had helped others through this very type of situation in the past: Pastor Peoples.

His pastor was more than willing to help Earnest take care of everything he needed to do in order to bring his mother home. Pastor Peoples took Earnest to classes at the hospital where he learned how to care for his mother. His pastor counseled with him, giving him resources and spiritual guidance to prepare him for this life change. It became obvious to Earnest, even before Pastor Peoples suggested it, that the logical thing to do was to move from his apartment into his mother's house: the house where he had grown up, the house with five bedrooms, the house across the street from what was now his church home. She would need him to be with her full-time to take care of everything she needed.

When she was ready to come home, Pastor Peoples took Earnest to the hospital to get her, and they brought her home. Pastor Peoples arranged for a nurse to come to the house three times a week. He took Earnest and his mother to the bank so she could put her son on her account, and to the lawyer's office so she could create a will and a living will, as well as put his name on the deed to her house. By this time, she was able to speak quietly – so unlike her former self – and write slowly, so there was no question that she was in agreement of the situation. As a matter of fact, it had been her idea. She wanted to take care of all of her business, and take care of her youngest son as well, as he was taking care of her.

Living in her house with her was easier than he ever would have thought, now that she couldn't yell at him any more — once he got things cleaned up and the house in balance. Her voice was now quiet, and she was reserved, no longer critical of everything he did, but, rather, thankful to him for stepping up to the plate and taking responsibility for her care. When he first went to her house, before she came home from the hospital, he was shocked to see that she was a food hoarder. She had hundreds of cans of food hidden in closets, and boxes of prepared food, most of them expired decades ago, as well as two upright freezers in the garage, packed with frozen food, most from the previous century. She had several cupboards stuffed with junk food, the kinds of food she had never let her children eat, that she had constantly told them was 'poison food full of sugar and salt.' He became convinced her stroke had been caused by her complete disregard of the selection of food she was putting in her body.

Earnest had been a strict health food eater for decades, so when he saw all the unhealthy food in his mother's house, he began to sort it into two groups. Anything packaged or canned that was dated before the expiration date, he put in bags to be donated to the homeless. Everything else, the quasi-food he didn't consider to be healthy, he put in the garbage, and over the course of four weeks, he was able to fit all of the junk food and old food into the single garbage can that was collected weekly by the sanitation department.

His next task was to get her house in order. While his mother had been a pretty good housekeeper, things were off balance. Some walls had lots of pictures, just put up any kind of way, and some walls were bare. The bookshelves were completely disorganized, and in the room she used as an office, she had saved receipts that went back to the 1960s. He spent a couple of weeks organizing and cleaning the house so when she came home, everything was in order for both of them. He also made the guest room on the main floor into his mother's bedroom, since she wouldn't be going up and down the stairs any more. The four bedrooms upstairs were now his domain. He chose the master bedroom as his room and was able to fit nearly all of his personal items from his apartment into it, with its nooks and crannies and two large closets. He set up the room that had been his childhood bedroom as his office, and he left the two bedrooms that had belonged to his brother and sister as they were, with their old beds and dressers still in place, if they wanted to come to visit. He didn't expect they would ever visit, as they never did, but he liked to be prepared, just in case they had a change of heart.

Earnest began to enjoy his life in his mother's house, with one exception: he missed going to church and seeing Sister Peoples. When his mother had first come home, Pastor and Sister Peoples came to the house several times with casseroles and fancy breads she had made. Pastor Peoples continued to make pastoral visits several times per month – after all, his mother had been a member of his congregation for nearly 30 years – but Earnest no longer went to church and interacted with Sister Peoples, and he missed that. Earnest treasured the time they had spent together, at church as well as during the car rides, and he had gotten to know little bits about her life and her dreams. She had made it apparent that Pastor Peoples was the love of her life and that she was sure it was God's plan for them to be together, but Earnest had a secret desire for her. It was not an unholy desire, it was more of a thought in the back of his mind that

Pastor Peoples was so much older than she was, and Earnest was closer to her age than her own husband was. She and Earnest enjoyed the same kind of music, even the same gospel and Christian artists, and they had both grown up in the same era, living with the same types of influences. In some ways, she really had been made for him, rather than for her husband.

He daily took his burden regarding this situation to God in prayer.

NICHOLAS
Then

The evening passed all too quickly. They went to her house for a few minutes so he could say hello to her parents, who were overjoyed to see him. He was happy they remembered him, and he was polite to them, yet anxious to leave their house. His only goal was to be alone with Mandy, but there were people everywhere they went. While Mandy was driving, she was babbling about this and that, and Nick didn't want to distract her.

She pulled her little car into his grandmother's driveway and stopped.

"Here we are," she said.

"Can we just talk for a few minutes?" he asked.

"Yeah, sure," she said. "I'm not in a hurry to get home. I can keep the car running, I have plenty of gas."

"It is really nice and warm in here," he said.

"The heater is strong, and there's not much room to heat," she said.

He wanted to take her hand, but he didn't know how to do it! He felt like he was on his first date. Actually, he was on his first important date. This was the date he had been waiting for all of his life, and it wasn't going the way he wanted it to go. He had so many important things he wanted to share with her. How could he say what he was feeling? How could he find out what she felt about him? He hadn't been able to bring it up, and he didn't know how to guide the conversation in that direction. She had monopolized the conversation for most of the night – he had let her, because he didn't know how to catch up after wanting to talk to her for the last ten years, ever since he had moved away from Yakima with his dad after 8th grade.

"Would it be all right if I kissed you?" he asked. Oh, no, that was not at all what he wanted to say! He did want to say that, but he had so many other things on his mind that he wanted to say first.

"Yes, that would be fine," she said, as if she were saying she would like fries with that burger.

He leaned over toward her as she leaned to him. The stick shift and the center console were in the way so he couldn't get as close to her as he wanted, but they did kiss. Her lips were soft and tender, although he couldn't help feeling that she was somewhat reserved. He was sailing high. All the old feelings came back to him and he was gaining the courage to ask her if she would like to share his life, to move to Boston, to be his girlfriend, to get engaged, to plan to spend the rest of their lives together. If he had had a ring with him, he would ask her to marry him. After all, she was the only girl for him, she always had been, and this kiss was all he needed to be reassured of that. He wanted to wrap his arms around her and pull her close to him. He didn't want the kiss to end. Here they were, finally, and he was working up the courage to pour out all of his feelings to her, to offer a place for her in his life, from now until forever.

He was ready now, and he was going to tell her everything that was on his mind. He drew in his breath to start, ready to pull her back into his life. He formulated exactly what he was going to say; but he wanted this kiss to last awhile longer. This was where he wanted to stay, with her.

She ended the kiss and pulled slowly away from him,

looking down. He could see in her eyes, or by her lack of eye contact, that she did not feel the same way about him, and he came crashing to the ground, out of the race before it even started. He was crushed. He felt hope draining out of him.

"I have a boyfriend," she confessed.

NICHOLAS
Now

Nick paced back and forth in the hallway near Mandy's hospital room. A man was in there talking to her, probably a minister or something. Nick was not used to not being the one in control of a situation. He had prided himself on always being in complete control, well, except for his shyness, which made him avoid social situations.

If he hadn't been so shy all those years ago, they would never have broken up in the sixth grade, and she wouldn't be here, now, in a coma, in this hospital bed. If, years later, he hadn't been so shy in the car at Christmas time, he could have told her how he felt about her, even before she told him she had a boyfriend, and she would have dumped that other guy to be his girl again. They would have gotten married as soon as he graduated from medical school, and she wouldn't have married someone else; and last week she wouldn't have been in a car accident to land here!

As soon as the man left her room, Nick went back in to see her. Was she finally awake? She was flat on her back, her eyes still closed.

"Mandy," he said softly, pulling up a chair near her bed, so he could be close to her, "I am so sorry. I let you down all those years ago, and the chain of events that ended up to be your life caused you to be here, right now. I am so sorry that I never came right out and told you that I love you."

He stared at her face.

He thought he detected the slightest movement in her face. She could hear him! He would have to resort to desperate measures.

He stood up and pulled the curtain around her bed so they could have some privacy.

"You know I love you, don't you?" he asked, settling in very close to her. "I know you do. I should have told you sooner, years ago. It's not too late for us to be together.

"We were made for each other. Remember when you told me about that Monkees song, 'We were made for each other,' and you said it was our song? I never actually heard that song, but you had it on one of your Monkees records, and it was your favorite song because it was written just for us, you and me. Wow, I haven't thought about that song in forty years!

"Mandy, come back to me. I really need you now. I have lost everything else in my life. No, that isn't exactly true. I have given up on everything else, because my life is an empty shell, just like that empty shell we found from that rifle that time on the school grounds. Do you remember it? We looked at it and wondered how something like that could do any damage to anything. Later on, I showed it to my dad and asked him about it, and he told me that it couldn't do any damage anymore because the gunpowder and the bullet were gone out of it.

"That has been my life without you, like an empty rifle shell, and the gunpowder and bullet have not been there. Please, Mandy, I have never been so open with anyone else in my entire life. Please, come back to me, and put the gunpowder and bullet back into my shell."

He thought that might sound strange to her, but he had to say something to bring her back to him! She was getting so close!

"What do you see?" he asked. All of his training and experience as a doctor had no meaning now. Right now, he needed some kind of miracle – and he didn't even believe in miracles. "I know you are looking at something. Just come back, into this room, and be here with me. I really need you. I need you more than anything."

He knew what would get her, what would bring her back, not only to today, but back to the memory of loving him. He leaned over and kissed her gently on the lips. He started to pull away from her, but instead, he closed his eyes and gave her a great kiss, pressing his lips firmly against hers, the way he had always wanted to kiss her. She had to feel the life coming from him, going into her, the warmth, the gunpowder getting ready to react. He was certainly feeling it.

He slowly ended the kiss and opened his eyes, sure that he would a reaction – but there was none. She continued to lie there, unmoving, as if he weren't even there.

He felt something inside of him break, again, and he realized it was his heart. He needed her, but even more, he needed her to respond to him.

MANDY

I am at the Mall, but I am not shopping. I am looking for someone.

I am thrilled to see some of my friends from first grade – Debbie and Janice and Julie and Heidi and Lisa. They are standing in line, waiting to buy something, laughing and joking around, looking so happy.

I approach the group and say hi. They have gotten so much taller than I am! I want to tell them how happy I am, too, because of Jesus and the life God has given me, but they just keep talking to each other while looking down at me.

They are talking about me, and I am right here! I smile, to shake it off, like my husband would do, but I feel hurt. They have never thought I was good enough. Someone does love me, someone thinks I am good enough, I know that, but can't remember who.

I clearly hear Carolyn say, in a man's voice, as she looks at me, but talking to the others, "She will never be able to take care of herself again."

They all laugh at me.

I feel like melting into the floor.

EARNEST
Then

Now that his mother was settled into her life at home with him, Earnest had a bit of freedom to be in other parts of the house, even when she was awake. He no longer had to stay by her bedside every moment at her beck and call. He was able to spend time in his office and get things organized in his computer. Someday, he was going to write a book, so he spent hours and hours typing notes and organizing ideas. Nothing was really coming together, but he liked to have a purpose and a plan, even if it seemed a little far-fetched. He wasn't in any hurry and he didn't need to write a book to earn money. He just liked the idea of thinking of himself as a writer. He thought about writing a blog, but he wasn't ready to type something and then have it out there immediately for the world to read. He chose every word carefully, considering every possible alternate meaning, not wanting anyone to ever be able to read into it something that wasn't there, something he didn't mean to be there.

As he sat at his desk, his horrid teenage years tried to haunt him. He had been so shy and had kept to himself, wanting to date a cute girl, but afraid to ask, when the boys started to call him 'homo.' Just because he was quiet, dressed in many layers, was kind of chubby, had a note that kept him out of P.E. (due to his back problem) and didn't have a girlfriend, they assumed he was looking for a boyfriend. Nothing could have been further from the truth, but he didn't have any way to prove it. He suffered every day at school from the name-calling and taunting, then at home from the tearing down by his mother. He could almost understand the whispered accusations by mean people who didn't know, who had no business talking about his family, who said his mother had given his father that fatal heart attack by her constant nagging and complaining. However, he remembered it a little differently. The nagging and complaining didn't start until after his father had passed away. Carolyn and Robert were ten years older than he, so they were able to stay away from the house for hours at a time, but Earnest was stuck with his mother every afternoon after school and nearly full time on weekends. When she finally started visiting churches in search of the place where she felt she belonged, Earnest had a couple of hours to himself on Sunday mornings, but the rest of the time he had to listen to her yelling. Even when he was all the way upstairs in his room, he could hear her irritating voice drilling into him.

Now he didn't have to listen to her yelling anymore, because she either couldn't or wouldn't raise her voice. She had gone through a transformation when she had her stroke, so now she was much quieter – and much more pleasant to be around. Sometimes she looked at him as if she were afraid he would treat her the way she had treated everyone else: with anger, with resentment, with an air of being better than anyone. He could not treat his mother that way, because he wasn't like that. He didn't have those qualities inside him, so they couldn't come out of him. He was full of thankfulness, love, and hope that each day and each opportunity would be better than the last. Inside him he now held the attitude of David: "This is the day that the Lord has made; I will rejoice and be glad in it." He had made the decision shortly after joining the church, to trust God to make every day a good day, and he was kind of amazed that each day did turn out to be a good day for him.

He sat at his desk, staring out the window at the church

building across the street. From here he could see the new roof and the two very high spots that had been missed when volunteers were painting the outside of the building. It really was a beautiful church, a nice off-white color with brown trim (one member referred to it as latte-colored with mocha trim) and a high steeple.

A car pulled into the pastor's parking space and he was delighted to see that it was Sister Peoples. She got out of the car and took a vacuum cleaner out of her trunk. She had a full bag of something over her shoulder as she pulled the vacuum to the front door and unlocked it. She adjusted her load and took it all inside the church. She didn't have the boys with her this time, the first time he had ever seen her without them.

Earnest had never thought about who cleaned the church, but it broke his heart to see his pastor's wife doing it. Shouldn't someone else be there to do the dirty work? Did she do this every Saturday, or was this a one-time thing? He sat staring at the church for a long time, angry that she would be the one to have to do this kind of work. He knew Pastor Peoples visited sick and shut-ins on Saturdays, because often when he made his rounds, he stopped to see Earnest's mother, and he couldn't expect the pastor of the church to be the one to clean it. Why wasn't someone else cleaning it? Someone else should be doing it! Earnest couldn't be the one, because he couldn't leave his mother alone in the house. He continued to stare out the window until finally Sister Peoples came out of the church, dragging the vacuum cleaner behind her. He watched her as she seemed to struggle to lift it into the trunk, but he caught a glimpse of a smile on her face. She wasn't mad about what she had to do. She was doing it with a smile!

He became aware that darkness was falling. He had been sitting in his office for more than two hours without doing a thing! He hurried down the steps to see if his mother needed anything. She would soon be getting hungry. It was time for him to start fixing dinner.

EARNEST
Now

When Earnest returned to the room, he forced himself to be bold enough to say what was in his heart. She couldn't know how he felt about her if he didn't make it known.

"You know why I couldn't come back to the church, don't you? No one could know what we did, and if I went into that church and saw you there, I would have to tell the truth to everybody. I would not be able to hide my feelings, and I have such strong feelings for you." He bit his lip, pulling up courage to continue.

"Only God knows how much you have touched my life and my heart and my soul, in a way that no one else ever has been able to. I feel a love and joy inside me whenever I think of you, and now, being here with you, I just want to be able to give some of that love and joy back to you."

He paused and examined Sister Peoples's face. She was laying there, as if her mind were miles away, and she could snap back here at any second. He looked across the room and continue talking to her.

"I remember something you taught your sons, and they told me. 'Kind words cost you nothing – but they are priceless to the hurting soul.' Your kind words to me have been priceless to me. I cherish every kind word you ever said to me, and you had no idea how much I was hurting. Your words were like a healing balm to me."

He glanced at her, positive that her mouth was now

just barely smiling! He felt as if he could bring her back to herself, if he just could say the right words.

"I know you can hear me, on some level. Maybe you want me to sing to you? I know, I will sing some of the songs we used to sing at church, and you can join in with me. Even if you can't sing out loud, you can sing with me, in your mind.

"One thing I always thought was really special about you, you have the best voice of anyone in the choir, but you never demanded to sing a solo. You should have had every solo, since you have the voice of an angel, but you so humbly let all the others sing, the ones who thought they were so good that they had to be featured. I always hoped we could sing a duet. Don't you think our voices would sound good together? Your angelic soprano with my deep baritone would really glorify God, don't you think?

"I'll start singing, and you can join in when you feel like it."

MANDY

Music is floating in and out of my mind, a song I recognize, one that brings peace to my soul. As I hear each word being sung, I know it is coming before it materializes, the pieces being put together in an amazing and familiar way. I can rest in this music as it is attempting to transport me to another place, a place I love.

I want to join in and sing. I want this music to be a part of me, to come from me, instead of coming through me, but I am not sure what to do. Somehow, it is bridging a gap from where I was then to where I am now, and I don't have to work so hard to finish all those tasks that have been stacking up all around me. The piles begin to melt away like ice cream on a hot day: something I thought wanted, something I thought I needed, but now I know, all I need is this music to continue and to never stop.

I will bless the Lord at all times... His praise shall continually be...

NICHOLAS
Then

During his final year in med school, Nick was renting a room in a large house in Boston, not far from the campus. A tall, very thin blond student moved into one of the other rooms and he began to see her around, in the kitchen, in the hallway, in the large drawing room where the student residents went to study. The first time he saw her, he despised her, because she was the opposite of Mandy. Mandy was petite and dark, with a round face, and this lady was angular, with a sharp nose, and her arms seemed to stretch clear across the room. Nick did his best to avoid her, but she was always there.

One evening while he was studying for an exam, she approached him boldly.

"I heard through the grapevine that your name is Nick, and you are in med school," she announced.

Nick nodded uncomfortably.

"I am Tess." She thrust her hand in his direction and he shook it gently, wishing she would just go away.

"Nice to meet you," he mumbled.

"Well, it's about time, don't you think?" she asked with a wink. "Can you believe it? I just passed the bar! I took the test today for the first time, and I passed!"

"You are a lawyer?" he asked, surprised. He had figured she was more the cheerleader type.

"I will be, before you know it," she said, smiling.

He had to admit, she did have a nice smile. But her teeth were somewhat crooked, not perfectly straight like Mandy's.

"Congratulations," he said, trying to remember his manners. "I have a big exam—"

"Which is why we should go out and celebrate!" she shouted.

Nick glanced around the room, and this was the first time it had been devoid of people.

"Really, I can't," he began.

"Of course you can!" she insisted. "Come on! I need you to come and celebrate with me!"

Nick began to feel uneasy, so he stood to his feet. He was barely an inch taller than she.

"I'm sorry, I can't go," he said, avoiding looking at her eyes, which were about level with his.

"Don't be a party pooper!" she said.

Nick was not fond of that phrase, so he grabbed his books and ran to his room without another word.

The rest of the evening he was unable to study. He wasn't sure if that was because of his rudeness or hers. She had no right to intrude into his private world, his study time. On the other hand, she had just accomplished a great achievement, and she had no one to celebrate it with her. He stared at his books nearly all night and left out of the house early in the morning. He aced his exams that day and the next.

Two days later, he spotted Tess sitting in the drawing room, staring out the window. He approached her cautiously.

"Good afternoon," he said gently.

She turned to face him and smiled.

"How about if we try that celebration of yours right now?" he asked shyly.

Later she would tell their friends at every gathering, that was the moment she fell for him.

NICHOLAS
Now

As soon as the nurse left Mandy's room, Nick was right there. Here eyes were open! The nurse had put her in a sitting position and Mandy was staring straight ahead. She was making progress! Yet, she didn't turn to see her visitor. She seemed to be unaware that he had entered the room.

"Mandy? It's me, Nick. I'm here for you." He leaned into her line of sight, where he was sure she would be able to see him, even if she couldn't move her head.

She didn't move an eyelash.

"Can you hear me now?" He looked into her eyes, those beautiful brown eyes that were unfocused. "I love you, Mandy. I had to give up on the fake life I was living because you have always been the one I love. Mandy, Mandy, come back to me. Please come back to me so we can finish living our lives together, the way we started, way back when we were in the second grade.

"Mandy, all I have ever wanted, all my life, was for us to be together, for us to get married and make our life together. Ever since we were in the second grade, you have been the only girl I have ever wanted in my life. In the years that we were apart, I have thought about you constantly. I compared every girl to you, and none were like you."

He passed his hand in front of her eyes. She didn't blink, didn't change her gaze.

"When I finally realized you had gone on with your life,

I let myself get involved with Tess. She was the opposite of you, but she had some of your best features. She was funny, smart and beautiful. She was a lawyer. She was so nice to me. We dated for four years. We finally got married. I expected her to be more like you, but she was her own person. She wasn't like you.

"We had two beautiful daughters, Angela and Aubrey. Or, I should say, we *have* two beautiful daughters, who are nearly grown by now. I went through the act of being the perfect husband and father, but in my heart, I always knew there was someone better for me. I always knew you were out there, somewhere, and I imagined that you were thinking of me and wanting us to be together, waiting for me, somewhere.

"You had no idea what you were doing to me, but you ruined my marriage. After fourteen years together with Tess, I had to admit to myself that I didn't love her. I loved the image of her, poured into the mold of you. I did – I do – love our daughters, but it was all like a game. It wasn't the real life I wanted for myself.

"I left the hospital where I was working and I moved here, to Seattle, where I thought I could start over. I knew you were still somewhere in the Northwest, and I thought maybe I could find you. I got a job working in this very hospital. I guess I lived in a sort of dream world, where I was expecting you to one day just walk back into my life, and we would continue our lives together.

"A couple of years ago, I moved to California and got a job in a smaller hospital. I bought a beautiful house for us, and I have been waiting for you to come back into my life, knowing you would feel like you belonged there, with me.

"As much as I love you, as much as I want you, and have waited for this moment, I have to admit to you as well as to myself, it has all been a fantasy. Tess was not you, and I was not fair to her to expect her to be you. I do love my daughters. I love them so much.

"And I do love you, more than you could ever know. But this is not what I have been waiting for all of my life. I have not come to this point to take care of an invalid. I want to live with you as your husband, not as your caretaker. I am sorry, but I just can't do it. I don't know if you will ever be able to walk or talk again, or if you will even know who I am. They will soon be discharging you from the hospital, and I can't take you home like this. You will be better cared for in a care facility where they can be with you all the time and monitor your needs. I am so sorry.

"If you can just speak or give any indication that you know who I am, and that you want to be with me, we might have some hope of a life together. But I just can't take you home without your consent, without some word from you that this is what you want.

"I wouldn't be able to take you to that house anyway, not in this condition. It has three stories, and it wouldn't work out to just keep you on the second floor all the time - unless you can give me a word. I can always sell that house, my house, and buy a house for us, our house, where we can live together.

"I'm not closing the door here, I am just asking you for a word or a sign. Can you do that? Can you blink for me? Can you squeeze my hand? Can you move your little finger and let me know that you are coming back to me? Can you give any indication that you know I am here?"

He, as a doctor, had dealt with this type of situation in a professional way, but now it was personal, happening to him. Any advice that he might have given to his patients or to the families of his patients was not relevant in his situation. He couldn't think of anything except getting Mandy to regain consciousness so they could finally start their life together. That was the only thing that mattered to him now.

He examined her face for any sign of movement. He held onto her hand, trying to will her to move, even a tiny bit. He wanted so badly for her to respond to him that when she didn't, he felt the tears come to his eyes. This was his last chance with her. He wouldn't be able to visit her in a nursing home, week after week, looking and hoping for some improvement. He would have to leave tomorrow, to go back to work, and Mandy would be sent to a care facility. He turned away from her, not letting himself face her, as the tears slowly slid down his face.

A nurse came in the room to check Mandy's numbers. Nick couldn't let her see him cry, so he stepped out of the room.

Neither Nick, ashamed of himself for crying, nor the nurse, busy with her job, noticed the single tear slip from Mandy's eye, down the side of her face.

MANDY

I am watching a movie, and I am in the movie. It is a love story, one of those romantic movies that my boys, including my husband, don't like to watch; so, I only get to see this kind of movie when I am home alone.

A familiar man is talking to me – the movie me – and I need to respond, but I don't know the script. He is telling me he loves me. He is handsome and he is gentle; yet he is just an actor saying his lines. I don't know him, except from the movies I have seen, and he doesn't know me. He is putting a lot of emotion into it, but I know he is just acting. As I watch myself on the screen, I want to answer him honestly.

His performance is touching. I feel like crying, because I can't answer him the way I want to answer. I must stick to the script.

Where are my lines? Why am I not allowed to tell him that I love him?

JAMIE
Now

Jamie watched the nurse leave Amanda's room, and he knew this might be his final chance to talk to her.

"Amanda, I wish I could take you home with me. I have always wanted to be with you. You were my best friend for so many years. You were the first girl I ever loved, even though I never had the nerve to tell you.

"It's funny, now that I don't even know if you can hear me or not, I am not afraid to tell you everything. I guess it's partly because I think you can't even hear me, so I'm a little braver around you, and partly because you can't answer and burst my bubble, the dream I have of us being together, now I can finally say all the things I've always wanted to tell you. But really, these are things I do want you to know.

"Wait, can you hear me? If you can, just give me a sign, any kind of sign that you can hear me, and that you know I am here?"

Amanda didn't move. She had that almost-smile on her face, the same one she always had, back in school. She appeared to be sleeping. Shouldn't he be able to wake her up?

He looked around to see if anyone was watching. He was the only one in the hospital room with Amanda, and no one was looking in the door. He reached down, through all the tubes and stuff, and put one hand on each of Amanda's shoulders. He shook her, gently at first, then harder.

"Wake up!" he insisted, not too loudly, though. He didn't want to attract any attention. He recalled his dad telling him, years ago, that sometimes unorthodox methods worked with unusual medical cases. He shook her a little harder. She did not respond.

He glanced out the door again. No one was paying any attention to him or this room. He moved his hand down to her side, just under her arm, and began to tickle her. She had always been so ticklish - this had to do the trick! He laughed a little, in anticipation of the response he was expecting from her. He leaned his face down close to her face, to see if she was even kind of smiling, or reacting to the tickling. His lips brushed against her cheek, the most delicate kiss he could share.

"What are you doing to her?" a male orderly asked, coming into Amanda's room.

Jamie quickly pulled his hands away from her.

"Nothing," he said, aware of how guilty he must sound.

"Well, you have to be careful around beautiful women who are in a coma," the orderly said.

"Yes, thank you," Jamie responded, nodding in agreement. "I know."

"Are you her husband?" he asked.

Jamie's heart leaped a little, wishing he could say that he was. "No, not yet," he said with a smile. He would ask her to marry him as soon as she regained consciousness.

"Then I need to ask you to leave the room while we check a couple of things," the orderly said.

"Yeah, sure," Jamie answered, going out into the hallway. If he had just had a couple more minutes, he knew he could have gotten to Amanda. She was right there, and he knew he could bring her back to herself. She wasn't like Brandy.

He walked down the hall, trying to not inhale the awful hospital smells that reminded him of his childhood, the days and weeks and years he had spent wandering the hospital halls while his dad was working. He was hungry, but he had promised himself long ago that he would never again eat another hospital meal, not after years of dinners in the hospital cafeteria in Yakima.

No, he thought, Amanda was not at all like Brandy.

JAMIE
Then

"You big liar!" Brandy shouted at Jamie, stumbling onto the sofa. "You never did love me! All you ever think about is your precious Amanda!"

"I haven't even seen her in, like, 25 years," Jamie protested.

"Yeah, and who has been here all this time for you?" Brandy yelled. Jamie could tell by the slur that she had been drinking again. "Who washes your clothes and who cleans your house and who cooks your dinner, every night, and who has been doing all that for all these years?"

"I wouldn't exactly call this house clean," he said softly, not wanting to fight with her again. "And when was the last time you cooked anything besides rock cocaine?" he added, not loud enough for her to hear.

"I do everything for you and all you want is your fantasy girlfriend," she pouted. "You don't even care about me."

"What is this about?" Jamie asked. He had come home from work to find Brandy intoxicated again. Ever since her son, Chris, had died from an overdose of a combination of drugs nearly three years ago, Brandy had gone off the deep end, drinking and taking drugs to hide from her pain. In the process, she had lashed out at Jamie, blaming him for everything. One Christmas, years ago, he had received a Christmas card from Amanda and her family, and he made the mistake of telling Brandy that Amanda had been his best friend in junior high. Brandy didn't say anything at the time, but after Chris died, whenever she was loaded, which was most of the time, she started in with her jealousy act.

It was true that Jamie did think of Amanda often, but not as a real alternative to his mistake of a life, more as a fantasy escape, the way other guys were always talking about what they would do if they won the 33-million-dollar lottery. Amanda was his lottery, a slight sliver of hope in the back of his mind, but not anything he ever really expected.

"Look, why don't you just go upstairs and relax?" Jamie suggested, reaching over to help her get off the sofa.

"Why, so you can call your girlfriend?" Brandy shouted accusingly.

"No, because you have had too much to drink, and you need to get some rest," Jamie said.

"Rest, rest, rest! That's all I do is rest!" she complained. "I am really tired, though," she admitted. "Do we have any more of those sleeping pills?"

"I think you already took them all," Jamie said. The sleeping pills had helped Brandy calm down and be able to sleep after Chris died, but when she began to rely on them, Jamie had called her doctor and asked him not to renew the prescription. When she discovered he had done that, she had gone into a deep depression and didn't say anything that made any sense for weeks. Later Jamie found an empty prescription bottle for sleeping pills, prescribed by another doctor.

Jamie had never been the dominant one in the relation-ship, but he knew he had to do something to help her and to help himself. He couldn't wait for Brandy to take the first step, because she was quickly slipping backwards, and he couldn't let himself be dragged down with her. Keeping her in bed most of the time was not the answer to this problem.

Every time she got out of bed, she got worse.

Jamie didn't know what to do. In his family, the way to deal with a problem had always been just to ignore it until it eventually went away, from his sister's unplanned pregnancy, which caused her to move away from home, to his dad's heart attack when he was at home alone the day after Jamie graduated from high school, which resulted in his death.

"I'm going to bed," Brandy announced. Jamie liked the idea of her being out of sight for the rest of the evening, so he helped her to her feet and up the stairs to their room.

Jamie was shocked by the condition of the room. Besides clothes being in piles everywhere, the chair and a nightstand were overturned. The mattress was almost halfway off the box springs, shoved onto the floor. The sheets were twisted into a rope across the mattress, the pillows nowhere to be seen. Jamie hadn't been in the bedroom for at least a week, but he had an idea how it had come to be in this condition.

"Thank you and good night," Brandy said, falling onto the mattress, before Jamie had a chance to pull it back onto the box springs. She immediately began snoring loudly, so Jamie backed out of the room and closed the door. He would have to sleep on the couch again tonight.

The next morning when he went to check on her, she was unresponsive. He tried to awaken her, but she was out completely. He called 9-1-1 and the ambulance arrived within five minutes. They transported her to the hospital, where she was pronounced dead on arrival. Apparently, sometime during the night, she had found more sleeping pills and taken a dose which was lethal when mixed with the amount of alcohol she had consumed.

In a way, her death was a relief to Jamie, after so many years of dealing with her addictions and the drama that came along with them: the shouting, the over-dramatized reactions to every situation, the embarrassment when she played out in public. In another way, he really missed her, because in between binges, she was the nicest, most loving person he had known as an adult. She had accepted him just the way he was. She had nearly forced herself into his life, just because she liked him, and she had made his life cheerful and exciting. She had gone all-out with Christmas decorations and birthday celebrations, two American traditions that had been all but ignored in his home while he was growing up, and he had enjoyed coming home to the Christmas music, the gingerbread houses, the giant tree in the tiny living room, and the little Christmas village that took over the dining room table.

He walked through the house, surveying the damage Brandy had done during this final drunken episode. The kitchen was a wreck, but mostly just garbage strewn all over the counters, table and floor. That would be easy enough to clean up. He saw the milk container sitting on the floor and realized he should probably get rid of any food he could find and go shopping for new food that wasn't spoiled.

He sat on the only kitchen chair that wasn't broken. What did he know about planning a funeral? Or, no, he needed to call Brandy's mother and tell her about Brandy's passing. He had no idea what to do first. He hadn't eaten since some time yesterday, and he couldn't even tell if he was hungry or not. His brain wasn't working, but he didn't know why. He hadn't gotten high or drunk in more than ten years, so why was his brain stalling on him like this?

Although the day was warm, he began shivering. What was he doing? He had to get his brain in gear! He had been so logical, so organized, on his part of this relationship. Brandy had been the crazy one, the wild one, the one who brought a different kind of spirit into his life. He had held down a job, made the house payments, paid all the bills, made sure they had normal food to eat in the house, done all of the cooking, and kept charge of the bank account. He had taken care of business, and he had taken care of her while she was on her highs and lows, while she had all the fun. Yet she was the one who had brought fun into his life, years after he admitted to himself that he could no longer wait for Amanda to reappear in his life.

Where was Amanda now? She had been there for him in junior high, but since then, she had never come to him when he needed her support. He needed some kind of guidance now, or at least a friend to talk to. Would she even remember him? Oh, of course she would. She was the one who reached out to him with her Christmas cards. Maybe he could find one of the cards and her phone number. If he could talk to her, even for a few minutes, he would know what to do.

Well, that was not a good idea, because he was sure that Brandy had burned all of the Christmas cards Amanda had sent. Amanda-Mandy. Brandy-Mandy. Had he subconsciously hooked up with Brandy because her name rhymed with Amanda's nickname?

Would he ever see Amanda again? He would! He would find her!

EARNEST
Now

Earnest hurried down the hall of the hospital. He hadn't meant to take a nap in the hospital cafeteria, but his lack of sleep over the past few days had not given him an opportunity to stay awake any longer. He had been away from Sister Peoples for at least five or six hours, maybe more.

As he approached her room, one of the friendly male nurses was just stepping into the hall. He smiled broadly when he saw Earnest.

"Her eyes are open!" he said, as if congratulating Earnest for something he had done.

"She's awake?" he asked incredulously, both excited and disappointed, since he had hoped to be there at the moment she awakened, so he would be the first person she saw.

"Well," the nurse said, in a sort of feminine way, "she's not exactly awake yet, but she did open her eyes. Her doctor said she's out of the coma, but she is still in a semi-comatose state. She might be able to eat, we will find out about that later, but she isn't talking, and she isn't moving her limbs or anything."

"That's wonderful!" Earnest said, truly thankful that his prayers were being answered. He couldn't help himself – he hugged the nurse. He quickly backed off, embarrassed by his uncontrolled emotion.

"Yes, and what's more, she is going to be discharged either tomorrow or the next day," the nurse continued.

"Where is she going?" Earnest asked, puzzled. "Who is going to take care of her?"

"Well," the nurse said, as if he were getting ready to share some gossip, "I heard that she will be sent to one of the local nursing homes, since no one in her family has come forward to claim her. We haven't been able to locate any of her relatives, unless, of course, you are related to her?"

"Not yet," Earnest said, not entirely sure what he meant by that. "How long do you think it will be before she gets better, or, back to her old self?"

"Well, I am not a doctor, so I can't really say," the nurse said, "but there is always hope."

"Yes, that's for sure," Earnest agreed, nodding happily. All she needed was some time to heal, time to recover, time to get her facilities back. "We can always have hope. Can I go in and see her?"

"Of course!" the nurse answered.

Earnest went into the hospital room and saw Sister Peoples, propped up so she was in a sitting position. Her eyes were open, but she had a blank stare, like the one his mother used to get when he had parked her wheelchair in front of the TV for too long.

"Hi, Sister Peoples," he said, moving into the space where she was looking. She was so beautiful, like an angel sitting there in a hospital bed. She looked so peaceful, not scared or lost, but simply at peace with her situation. He knew she could come out of this at any second. She would blink her eyes and shake her head a little, and she would be her old self again.

She just needed a little nudge. He moved over, close to the bed, and glanced out the door to be sure no one was looking. He bent down near her face and kissed her briefly on the cheek. Then, after another quick glance out the door, he moved in a bit closer, and he kissed her on her lips, the prince that would finally awake Sleeping Beauty.

His heart leaped in his chest with anticipation. This could be it!

She did not react, but he held onto his hope. One thing he had learned from her a long time ago was to always have hope.

MANDY

I am really enjoying this wonderful party. Even though I don't drink alcohol, I have a drink in my hand, as I am moving through the crowds. The music is pleasant, rock music I enjoyed way back in the 1970s, during the previous century when I was a teenager. The conversation of the crowds comes at me in waves, getting louder, then quiet, then louder again. I catch bits of conversation, snippets here and there, and everything seems so logical to me. I can even understand a group of people speaking Spanish, and I think, in Spanish, of witty things I can add to what they are saying, if I choose to join them. I choose not to join them. I see a couple of my old classmates from high school that I haven't seen since our last reunion, but I don't feel like getting into their business right now, either. I may come back this way again a little later.

I set my drink on a coffee table. I don't want to drink it and can't even remember how it got in my hand in the first place. A waiter comes by with a tray holding a variety of chocolates; that is more my style, more than wine or any type of alcoholic drink. I ponder for a moment, why must it be on TV that the adults have to drink to have a good time or to get over a bad time? I feel that is a bad influence on our society, as well as a reflection of our society, but as I look at the ones who are gathered here tonight, I don't see anyone who may agree with my point of view, as they are all drinking.

A man comes over to me and stands beside me.

"Are you ready to go?" he asks. I don't know who he is. I assume he is asking me if I am ready to leave with him.

I try to answer him and tell him I can't go with him (because I don't know who he is?) but my throat is so dry, I can't get any words to come out of it. I want my husband to join me, but I have no idea where he is.

I begin to cough, covering my mouth with my hand. I notice that my hand looks very odd. I open it and turn it so I can see my palm. My hand looks kind of greenish, and I can see the bones inside, a bright pink under my translucent green skin. This is how I know this is a dream.

I nod to myself, understanding everything now. I am ready to go, from this dream, on to the next. But how do I get there? I am not sure how to wake myself up, but I am ready to change the channel now and go into another dream.

It isn't happening. I am still here, so I sit on a bar stool and watch the party pass in front of my eyes. I have no reason to try to fly away from this party or from this dream. Although it is not fantastic, it is pleasant enough. I'll just wait.

EARNEST
Now

"I never had a chance to tell you this before, but I have always thought you were extraordinary. From the first day I met you, when you picked me up at my house, I saw something unique in you, something that no one else has. You have held a special place in my heart, a place that has always been there, just for you." Earnest pulled the chair close so he could talk to Sister Peoples without having to raise his voice at all, and she would be able to hear him.

"You probably didn't notice that I was watching you. I couldn't help myself. Even when I wasn't looking at you, I was watching, from the corner of my eye, and listening to the sweet sound of your voice. I don't know how you could always be so nice to everyone, even the ones who didn't care anything about you or anything about God, and even the women who came to church because they had a crush on your husband. I know you were aware of it, and I really admired the security you had in your marriage. You knew he loved you. I know he still loves, and he is looking down from heaven, watching you."

Earnest had to stop and wipe a tear that his eye could not contain. He prayed within, asking for God to give him the strength to do what he needed to do.

"I would love to have the boldness and security in a relationship that you had with him. You know that I have never been very comfortable around people, but you are different. I always want to be around you. Sometimes when I was with you, I couldn't look at you because I felt tears coming to my eyes. I always feel so emotional when I am around you. You just have that effect on me, because, you probably don't even know it, you send out rays of love."

JAMIE
Now

Jamie watched a man come out of Amanda's room and walk over to the elevators. He wasn't dressed like a doctor, but he could be some kind of administrator or a social worker or something, all dressed up like that. Jamie wondered who he was, but he didn't want the man to see him go into Amanda's room. He waited until the man entered the elevator and the doors closed before he went to Amanda's room.

He immediately noticed a difference in Amanda. She was now in a reclining position, not flat on her back, and her eyes were open!

"Amanda!" Jamie whispered loudly. "You came back!" He was so excited that her eyes were open, he figured she must be awake. But she was just staring straight ahead. She looked like she wasn't seeing anything. "Can you hear me? It's me, Jamie! I'm here for you!"

"She can't hear you," the grouchy nurse said, as she came into Amanda's room.

Jamie shook his head. He didn't believe her. She didn't know what she was talking about. This was Amanda, and he knew she *could* hear him!

"She might look like she's awake, sitting there with her eyes open like that, but they just finished running a whole series of tests, and she's just a nice house with nobody home. She could stay like this forever. Don't get your hopes up, Bub. You might as well go home. She's going to be sent to a nursing home – oh, *excuse* me, a *care facility* – probably tomorrow. We need the bed space, and she doesn't need to be here anymore." She picked up the clipboard and made some notes, looking up at the monitor that was still connected to Amanda.

Jamie looked at the nurse in astonishment. Here was Amanda, miraculously awake, after all this time in a coma, and the grouchy nurse was telling him that she was going to be discharged from the hospital and sent to a nursing home? No, that couldn't be possible. She was too young to be sent to a place with old people, and she *was* going to get better. She was going to get back to normal. She just needed some more time to heal, a little more time to snap out of it.

"Unless you are going to take her home," the nurse snapped, as she left the room.

Yes, yes, he could take her home... but to her home? He didn't even know where she lived. No, he could take her to his home... but his old house had steps up to the porch and a narrow stairway up to the bedrooms. Could she walk? How long would he have to take care of her before she could take care of herself – and him?

He thought about the years he had taken care of Brandy, in her drunken and high states, which still felt like a burden to him, even though she had been gone for a while now, how he always had felt he was just a few steps behind where he should be. He was just now starting to get his house in order and his life in order.

All he had ever wanted in his life was Amanda, but not like this. Granted, even at her best, she would not be exactly the same as she was when they were best friends as kids. She had grown up and had been an adult for quite a while now, but she was still the same Amanda. He didn't know if he could take care of her full-time. He did have his job, which, thankfully, he now was on a mini-vacation, but he would have to go back to work, and if Amanda stayed like this, who would take care of her while he was at work?

This was just his luck. He had come here, or been brought here by luck, with a hope that he and Amanda would finally be together for life, and now his luck had turned on him. She was in no condition to come to his home like this. Maybe she would get better after a couple of weeks. Maybe she could go to the nursing home, or the care facility for a little while, and she would get better, come out of this semi-comatose state and they could live happily after. Maybe if he took her home, to his house, she would snap out of this state when she saw how much he loved her. He had finally confessed it to her, so maybe she now knew, and she was getting ready to come home with him.

He had to go back to work in Yakima in a couple of days. He didn't have much time to make a decision on what to do with Amanda, since she had to leave the hospital tomorrow.

Maybe he could figure it out.

NICHOLAS
Now

Nick was frustrated, disappointed. Mandy's eyes were open, but she was not herself. She would, at least at this point, need full-time care. Nick needed her to be strong and smart and funny. He wanted her to be able to take care of his needs. They should be equals, not doctor and patient.

He returned to her room to see if she had made any progress. She was in a sitting position, staring. Her eyes were open, yet what could she see?

"Mandy, I'm back," he said cheerfully. He paused, looking at her expectantly, but she didn't respond. How he longed for her to say, "Hi Nick! I'm back, too!"

"We can finally have a wonderful life together, you and I. You and I both know we were always meant to be together. I have a home prepared for us. You will like living in California. Or we don't have to stay there, we can live anywhere, as long as we are together."

He held her hand and closed his eyes. Was he trying to kid her, or himself? He felt like crying again. He figured this might be a good time to start praying.

EPILOGUE

I am sitting in a very nice house. It seems familiar to me. I am not sure where I am. I can't move my hands or feet. I feel like I am glued in one spot, glued to this chair. I can see and I can think, but I go from dream to dream and then I keep coming back to this place. Sometimes I am looking at a church where I used to go in another life. I don't know which life this is.

A good-looking man comes into the room carrying a tray of food. He has brought me food before. I think I know him, but he must be a part of this dream, this dream where I keep returning. His smile is very kind, and his mouth moves, but I can't make sense of the sounds he is making. I think I have taken up a different language, or has he?

He wants me to open my mouth to eat. If I really concentrate, I can make that happen. I don't want him to look at me this way, like he is worried, so I think about opening my mouth and he smiles. I don't recognize this taste, but the texture is pleasant. I can eat this. I focus on my mouth, opening and eating, and then the swallowing part. This task takes all of my effort, but the nice man looks happy. I must be doing the right thing. I don't like anyone to get mad at me.

I wonder where the children are. In one life, children ask me questions and I am able to help them. I don't see or hear them now. They must be in school.

I know I have a husband, but where is he? I can't recall the last time I saw him, or if that was this life or another life, but I know he exists, and I know he will be back home to me. He must be doing something important for someone. He is always busy. He helps everyone, even those people who think they can't help themselves. Maybe I have to go home from this place. I am not sure how to get there from here.

I hear some familiar sounds. I recognize it: Jesus music! I have heard this song before, and I know it, down inside me. The words take shape in my head and I can't quite put them together, but this is something that I know and like. It makes me feel calm inside to have this music hugging me as I sit in this beautiful, comfortable home.

The nice man puts a napkin to my face. I feel like he is trying to give me a kiss with the napkin. He is not my husband, but he is taking care of me. I want to smile at him, but I don't know if my mouth is curving up the right way. He smiles at me. He puts a warm, cozy something over my shoulders and looks into my eyes, moving his mouth again. I want him to know that whatever he put on my shoulders feels good, and now I am feeling nice and warm all over. I concentrate on forming my lips into a smile. He props up my feet on a little pillow. He sees me smiling and he stops what he is doing and smiles at me. He is so kind. He is treating me like I am a queen.

I wonder if he knows I was the Queen in Cinderella.

Available from Everlasting Publishing

<u>Novels by Dana Pride</u>
- » *Coma Talk*
- » *Vinnie Pinchey*
- » *Hope Continually*
- » *The Great Devastation Trilogy*
    - • *After the Great Devastation*
    - • *The Hidden City*
    - • *Immediate Search*
- » *So How is THAT a Bully?*
- » *The Red Cloak*
- » *Nightmares of Murder*
- » *No One Like You*
- » *Existing*
- » *All These Things*
- » *Kissing a Dead Man*

<u>Non-fiction books by Dana Pride</u>
- » *How to Get Fat Without Even Trying*
- » *What Really Happened in Mexico*
- » *We Choose our Memories:
  Sayings of the Young Folks*
- » *We Choose our Memories:
  Sayings of the Old Folks*

<u>Sermon books by Pastor W.F. Pride, Jr.</u>
- » *Volume 1 - God Wants You to Do His Will*
- » *Volume 2 - Everyone Needs Jesus*

Poetry books by Joseph Fram
- » *Joseph's Journey, Volume 1*
- » *Joseph's Journey, Volume 2*
- » *Joseph's Journey, Volume 3*
- » *Joseph's Journey, Volume 4*
- » *Joseph's Journey, Volume 5*
- » *Joseph's Journey, Volume 6*
- » *Joseph's Journey, Volume 7*
- » *Joseph's Journey, Volume 8*

Books by Steven Lowell-Martin
- » *Four Pounds of Pressure*
- » *Coptales: From the Penthouse to the Basement*
- » *Moses' Chisel*

Full-color books
- » *Baby Bugs' Best Time, by Katelyn Spurlock*
- » *Nathan is Nathan, by Jahla*
- » *Nathan Art: Autistic-Artistic, by Nathan*
- » *My Friend is Deaf, by Dana Pride*

Poetry book by Dana Fram
- » *Perceptions of Perfection: 66 Poems for a Rock Star*

All titles also available as e-books.

Everlasting Publishing
PO Box 1061
Yakima, Washington 98907
USA

http://everlastingpublishing.org